FAIRY TALES FROM
HANS CHRISTIAN ANDERSEN

A Classic Illustrated Edition

FAIRY·TALES·FROM
HANS ANDERSEN

A CLASSIC ILLUSTRATED EDITION

Compiled by
Russell Ash and Bernard Higton

PAVILION

First published in Great Britain in 1992 by
PAVILION BOOKS LIMITED
26 Upper Ground, London SE1 9PD

Conceived, edited and designed by Russell Ash & Bernard Higton.

Introduction copyright © 1992 by Russell Ash.

A CIP catalogue record for this book
is available from the British Library.

ISBN 1 85145 7240 (hbk)
ISBN 1 85145 9421 (pbk)

Printed and bound in Singapore by Kyodo

2 4 6 8 10 9 7 5 3

This book may be ordered by post
direct from the publisher. Please contact
the Marketing Department.
But try your bookshop first.

CONTENTS

HANS CHRISTIAN ANDERSEN
AND HIS ILLUSTRATORS

Hans Christian Andersen described his own life as a fairy tale, and it was certainly the stuff of make-believe. He was an uneducated boy from a poor family who was to rub shoulders with aristocrats and kings, and a shy adult who rose above his shortcomings to hold children spellbound with tales that have continued to enthral generations ever since. The enduring appeal of his stories has also resulted in editions containing some of the finest illustrations of the past 150 years.

Andersen was born in Odense, Denmark, in 1805, the son of a cobbler and a washerwoman. Despite his background and lack of education, Andersen's father encouraged his son's early interest in literature and drama. At the age of 14, Andersen convinced his mother to allow him to seek his fortune in Copenhagen, the capital of Denmark. A combination of determination and good luck led him to become first a singer and actor, then a dramatist — although an unsuccessful one — and finally a writer. His first book, aptly entitled *Youthful Attempts* (1822), sold just seventeen copies (with the remaining 283 being sold to a grocer for use as wrapping paper). But after extensive travels throughout Europe gathering material, his novel, *The Improvisatore*, was published in 1835 and was an immediate success. His

Top left: Hans Christian Andersen as portrayed by Arthur Rackham in his 'Fairy Tales' (1932).
Above: One of William Heath Robinson's vivacious illustrations to 'Elfin Mount' (1913).

Vilhelm Pedersen's classic illustrations for 'Thumbelina' and 'The Little Mermaid'.

Fairy Tales Told for Children, which appeared in the same year, was not immediately appreciated. But as he wrote more tales, his genius became internationally recognized, and within his lifetime he found himself acknowledged as the pre-eminent master of the fairy tale. He soon dropped the phrase "Told for Children" from the titles of his books, a clear sign that he was aiming to expand his readership to include adults. He explained that he was writing for children, but with the knowledge that their parents would be looking over their shoulders. Andersen broke new ground by writing in the language of everyday speech (which accounts for the stories' often unusual structure and the use of short, broken sentences), and he had a unique ability to read his stories aloud and to act them out. He clearly revelled in "singing for his supper", and, as a result, he became a popular guest of distinguished families throughout Europe.

Between 1835 and 1872, Andersen produced 156 *eventyr* (a Danish word that implies wonderful tales). His first collection was unillustrated, but the success of the stories led quickly to the appearance of illustrated editions. As their popularity spread, many notable illustrators tried to meet the challenge of illustrating the fantastic images Andersen conjured up in words. None

A drawing from Lorenz Froelich's early version of 'The Little Mermaid'.

was particularly distinguished until a German publisher persuaded Andersen to find a Danish artist to illustrate a German edition of his stories. The artist Andersen chose was the relatively unknown Vilhelm Pedersen, whose version appeared in German in 1848 and in Danish the following year. Gentle and sensitive, simple and unassuming, Pedersen admirably captured the appealing aspects of Andersen's prose, and continued to illustrate his work for the next ten years. After Pedersen's death in 1859, the role of "official" Andersen illustrator passed to Lorenz Froelich, who between 1867 and 1874 illustrated three volumes of a five volume set, concentrating on some of the less familiar stories and placing greater emphasis on the satirical and fantasy elements. In Denmark at least, Pedersen and Froelich became synonymous with Andersen.

Outside Denmark, numerous editions appeared as far away as India. Other editions containing simple woodcuts appeared in the 1860s, generally of unmemorable quality, until the arrival of Eleanor Vere Boyle. Inspired by the Pre-Raphaelites, "E.V.B.", as she signed herself, became one of the leading mid-Victorian female book illustrators and turned to Andersen's work in 1872, producing a dozen striking woodcuts designed to be hand-

coloured. In 1884, *Andersen's Fairy Tales* with 200 illustrations by the natural history artist Harrison Weir and others was published in London and New York. The fashion for illustrating single stories, rather than collections, also developed in the 1880s and 1890s.

In 1901 William Heath Robinson and his brothers Charles and Thomas Heath Robinson collaborated in creating black-and-white illustrations for *Fairy Tales from Hans Christian Andersen*. William Heath Robinson was later to return to Andersen, in 1913 producing one of the most beautiful of all illustrated versions, with exuberant colour plates and graphic line illustrations and silhouettes. The decorative artist Maxwell Armfield's *Faery Tales from Hans Andersen* was published in London and New York in 1910, followed the next year by Edmund Dulac.

During the Edwardian period, regarded by many as the "Golden Age" of children's book illustration, the sumptuous colour plate "gift books" of Heath Robinson, Dulac and others co-existed with those of simpler "nursery-style" illustrators responsible for versions aimed at very small children.

HONOR C · APPLETON ·

· It was the SNOW QUEEN ·

Top left: Anne Anderson's nursery-style image of 'The Storks' (1924).
Above: Honor C. Appleton's evocative Snow Queen (1922).

Above: Arthur Rackham's fantasy interior from 'Little Ida's Flowers'.
Top right: Danish artist Kay Nielsen's dramatic 'The Shepherdess and the Chimney Sweep'.

These included Mabel Lucie Attwell, who turned to Andersen more than once but produced her best collection in 1914, and Honor C. Appleton, whose version appeared in 1922. Harry Clarke's richly illustrated selection appeared in 1916 and an edition by Andersen's fellow-countryman Kay Nielsen (who was later to produce designs for Walt Disney's *Fantasia*) was published in 1924. The 1930s were notable for such illustrated editions as that of Jeannie Harbour, working in a distinctive Art Deco style, and the boldly colourful work of John Hassall in his *The Ugly Duckling*. Following a visit to Denmark in search of "local colour", Arthur Rackham's magnificent edition was published in 1932. And, since the Second World War, the illustration of Andersen has continued with numerous editions by such artists as Ernest Shepard (best known for his classic illustrations of Winnie the Pooh) in 1961.

For more than 150 years, not one year has passed without a new visual interpretation of Andersen's best-loved stories, a tradition that is gloriously celebrated in the following pages.

ONE DAY TWO SWINDLERS ARRIVED

THE EMPEROR'S
NEW CLOTHES

LONG ago there lived an emperor who was so
enormously fond of beautiful new clothes that he
spent all his money on dressing himself
up. He couldn't be bothered with his soldiers, or
with going to the theatre or driving out to the forest,
except to show off his new clothes. He had a robe for every hour of the
day, and just as you can say that a king is "in council", here they always
said, "The Emperor is in wardrobe."

In the big city where he lived, there were lots of nice things going on,
and plenty of visitors came every day. One day two swindlers arrived. They
spread the word that they were weavers and that they knew how to weave
the loveliest cloth imaginable. Not only were the colours and the pattern
unusually beautiful, but clothes sewn from this material had the remarkable
quality of being invisible to anyone who was not good at his job, or who
was intolerably stupid.

"Those clothes sound lovely," thought the Emperor. "If I wore them, I
could find out who in my kingdom is no good at his job, and I'd be able to
tell the bright people from the stupid ones. Yes, I must have that cloth
woven immediately." And he gave the two swindlers a great deal of money
so they could start on their work.

The two swindlers set up their looms and pretended to be working,
though there wasn't the least little thing on their looms. They kept asking
for the finest silks and the most magnificent gold thread, but they put it all
into their own bags and worked far into the night on the empty looms.

"I'd love to know how they're coming along with that cloth," thought
the Emperor, though his heart fluttered at the thought that anyone who was
stupid or incompetent in his work wouldn't be able to see it. He was sure
he needn't worry on his own account, but even so, he decided he would
first send someone to see how things were going. Everyone in town knew

what wondrous power the cloth possessed, and everyone was eager to see how incompetent or stupid his neighbour was.

"I'll send my honest old minister over to the weavers," thought the Emperor. "He'll be the best man to see what the cloth looks like, for he's bright, and no one attends to his job better than he."

So the trusty old minister went into the hall where the two swindlers were sitting working at the empty looms. "Oh, my goodness," he thought, opening his eyes wide. "I can't see anything!" But he didn't say a word.

The two swindlers invited him to come closer and asked him whether he didn't find the pattern beautiful and the colours lovely. Then they pointed to the empty loom, and the poor old minister opened his eyes still wider, but he couldn't see anything, for there was nothing there. "Good heavens," he thought. "Could it be that I'm stupid? I never thought I was. I mustn't let anyone find out. Could it be that I'm no good at my job? No, it would never do to tell anyone that I can't see the cloth."

"Well, aren't you going to say anything?" said one of the weavers.

"Oh, it's delightful, absolutely ravishing," said the old minister, peering through his glasses. "Just look at that pattern, and these colours! Yes, I shall definitely tell the Emperor that it has my approval."

"Ah, that's good to hear," said both the weavers, and then they described the colours and the cloth's remarkable pattern. The old minister listened carefully so as to be able to repeat their words when he got back to the Emperor – and so he did.

The swindlers demanded more money, more silk and more gold thread, which they said they needed for their weaving. But not a single strand found its way to the loom, for they put it all in their own pockets and went on as before, weaving on the empty loom.

Before long the Emperor sent another trusty official to see how the weaving was progressing, and to discover whether the cloth would soon be finished. But the same thing happened to him: he looked and looked, but as there was nothing there except the empty looms, he couldn't see anything.

"Isn't it a beautiful piece of cloth?" asked the two swindlers, showing him and describing to him the lovely pattern that wasn't there at all.

"I'm not stupid," thought the man. "So it must mean I'm not suited to my job. I'd better not let that be known." And so he praised the material he couldn't see and assured the weavers how delighted he was with the beauti-

"OH, IT'S DELIGHTFUL, ABSOLUTELY RAVISHING," SAID THE OLD MINISTER

ful colours and the lovely pattern. "Yes, it is absolutely ravishing," he said when he returned to the Emperor.

Everyone in town was talking about the magnificent cloth.

At last the Emperor decided to see the cloth for himself while it was still on the loom. Together with a group of chosen men, including the two worthy old officials who had been there before, he went to visit the cunning swindlers, who were now weaving with all their might, but without either thread or stitches.

"Isn't it beautiful?" said both the upright officials. "Just look, Your Majesty, what a pattern, and what colours!" And they pointed to the empty loom, for they believed that the others must surely be able to see the cloth.

"What on earth is this?" thought the Emperor. "I can't see anything. This is terrible. Am I stupid? Aren't I fit to be Emperor? That would be the most dreadful thing that could happen to me!" And so he said, "Ah, how beautiful! It has my most gracious approval!" And he nodded his satisfaction and looked at the empty loom; he wasn't going to say he couldn't see anything. All the courtiers accompanying him looked and looked, but with no more success than the others; yet, like the Emperor, they said, "Ah, how beautiful." And they advised him to wear these magnificent new clothes for the first time in the grand procession that was to take place the next day. "It's beautiful, gorgeous, splendid." The word spread from mouth to mouth, and everyone was delighted. The Emperor gave each of the swindlers a decoration for his buttonhole and the title of "Weaver by Appointment to His Majesty".

In the light of more than sixteen candles, the swindlers stayed up for the whole of the night before the procession. People could see they were hurrying to finish the Emperor's new clothes. They pretended to take the cloth from the loom; they made cutting movements in the thin air with huge pairs of scissors; they sewed with needles without thread; and finally they said, "There, now the clothes are ready."

The next day the Emperor, together with his most distinguished courtiers, went to the weaving room. Both the swindlers raised one arm up as though they were holding something, and said, "There, here are the trousers. Here is the coat. Here is the cloak." And so on. "It's as light as gossamer. You would almost think you hadn't anything on, but that is just the beauty of it."

"Yes," said the courtiers, but they couldn't see anything, for there was nothing to see.

"Would Your Imperial Majesty like to take off your clothes?" said the swindlers. "Then we can dress you in the new ones here in front of the mirror."

The Emperor took off all his clothes, and the swindlers acted as though they were handing him each new garment they were supposed to have sewn, and the Emperor turned and twisted in front of the mirror.

The Emperor walked in the procession beneath the lovely canopy

"Good Heavens, how well they suit him! And what a splendid fit!" said everyone. "What a design! What colours! It is indeed a gorgeous outfit."

Finally, the principal master of ceremonies announced, "The canopy to be held over Your Majesty in the procession is ready outside."

"Yes, well, of course I'm ready," said the Emperor. "Doesn't it fit beautifully?" And once more he turned around in front of the mirror, for he wanted everyone to see that he was taking a good look at himself in his new clothes.

The lords-in-waiting who were to carry the cloak fumbled with their hands along the floor as though they were picking it up. Then they walked along with their hands up in the air, for they dare not let it be noticed that they couldn't see anything.

The Emperor walked in the procession beneath the lovely canopy, and all the people in the street and in the windows said, "Aren't the Emperor's new clothes absolutely wonderful? What a lovely train there is to his robe. Doesn't it fit him beautifully?" No one wanted it to be noticed that he couldn't see anything, for in that case he would either have been very stupid or not fit for his job. None of the Emperor's other costumes had ever been such a success.

"But he hasn't got anything on!" said a little child. "Good heavens, listen to the little innocent," said the child's father. And people whispered the child's words to one another until at last the whole populace roared, "But he hasn't anything on!" The Emperor felt his blood turn cold, for he sensed they were right, but he thought to himself, "I must go through with the procession now." And the lords-in-waiting walked after him, carrying the train that simply wasn't there.

"BUT HE HASN'T GOT ANYTHING ON!" SAID A LITTLE CHILD

THUMBELINA

THERE was once a woman who very much wanted to have a little child, but she had no idea where to get one. So she went to an old witch and said to her, "I would so dearly love to have a little child. Won't you tell me where to find one?"

"Yes, I can do that all right," said the witch. "Here's a barleycorn. It's not the sort you find growing in the farmer's field or give the hens to eat. Now, plant it in a flowerpot, and then you'll have a surprise."

"Thank you," said the woman and gave the witch twelve silver coins. Then she went home and planted the barleycorn, and instantly a lovely flower appeared. It looked just like a tulip, except that the petals were tightly closed, as though it were still in bud.

"That's a pretty flower," said the woman and kissed its beautiful red and yellow petals. But just as she kissed it, the flower made a popping sound and opened. It was a real tulip – that was obvious now – but on a little green chair in the middle of the flower sat a tiny girl. She was sweet and pretty, and no bigger than your thumb, and so the woman called her Thumbelina.

She was given a pretty lacquered walnut shell for a cradle, blue violet petals for a mattress, and a rose petal for her quilt. In the day-time she played on the table, where the woman put a plate surrounded by a ring of flowers, all with their stems sticking into the water. Thumbelina was allowed to sail in a big tulip petal from one side of the plate to the other, and she had two white horsehairs to row with. It was lovely to watch. She could sing, too, in the prettiest, sweetest voice ever heard.

One night, while Thumbelina lay in her beautiful bed, a hideous toad jumped in through the window, where a pane had been broken. She was an ugly toad, all big and wet, and she jumped straight down on to the table where Thumbelina lay asleep under the red rose petal.

"She'd be a lovely wife for my son," said the toad,

THUMBELINA WAS LEFT BEHIND WEEPING ON THE GREEN LEAF

and she took hold of the walnut shell in which Thumbelina was sleeping, and jumped off with her through the window and down into the garden.

There was a big, broad stream flowing in the garden, and its edge was marshy and muddy. This was where the toad lived with her son. He was horrible and ugly, too, and he looked just like his mother. "Croak, croak, croak," was all he could say when he saw the pretty little girl in the walnut shell.

"Don't talk so loud, or she'll wake up," said the old toad. "She could still run away from us, for she's as light as swan's down. We'll put her out in the stream on one of the broad water-lily leaves; it'll be like an island to her, for she's so tiny and light. She won't be able to run away from there. Then we'll smarten up the best room down under the mud where you're going to set up your home."

Growing out in the stream were many water-lilies with those broad green leaves that look as though they are floating on the water. The leaf that was furthest out was also the biggest of all, and the old toad swam out and placed the walnut shell with Thumbelina inside on the leaf.

Poor little Thumbelina woke quite early in the morning, and when she saw where she was she began to weep, for there was water all around the green leaf and there was no way of getting ashore.

The old toad was down in the mud, decorating her room with reeds and yellow water-lilies. It was going to be really nice for the new daughter-in-law. Then she swam with her ugly son out to the leaf on which Thumbelina was standing. They wanted to fetch her sweet little bed, as it was to be put in the bridal chamber before she went there herself. The old toad curtseyed deep in the water before Thumbelina and said, "This is my son. He's going to be your husband, and you're going to have a very comfortable home down in the mud."

"Croak, croak, croak," was all the son could say.

Then the toads took the pretty little bed and swam off with it, but Thumbelina was left behind weeping on the green leaf. She didn't want to live with the ugly toad or have her hideous son for a husband. The little fishes swimming nearby must have seen the toad and heard what she said, and so they poked their heads up to have a look at the little girl. As soon as they caught sight of her they thought how pretty she was, and it hurt them to think she was to go down to that ugly toad. No, it should never happen!

A PRETTY WHITE BUTTERFLY FLUTTERED AROUND HER

They crowded together in the water around the stalk of the leaf on which she was standing, and gnawed through it with their teeth; and then the leaf floated off down the river, carrying Thumbelina far away, where the toad couldn't go.

Thumbelina sailed past many villages, and the little birds perched in the bushes saw her and sang, "What a pretty little girl." The leaf carrying her drifted further and further away; and that is how it happened that Thumbelina went abroad.

A pretty white butterfly fluttered around her, and at last he settled on the leaf, for he liked Thumbelina very much. Thumbelina was happy, for now the toad couldn't reach her, and it was lovely where she was sailing. The sun was shining on the water like the purest gold. Then she took her belt, tied one end to the butterfly and fixed the other end to the leaf. It floated along more quickly now, and so did she, for she was standing on the leaf.

Just then a big May beetle flew by and noticed her, and straight away he grabbed her slender waist with his claw and flew up in the tree with her. But the green leaf drifted downstream and the butterfly flew with it, for he was tied to the leaf and couldn't get loose.

How scared poor Thumbelina was when the May beetle flew up into the tree with her, and yet she was more upset about the lovely white butterfly she had tied to the leaf. If he couldn't free himself now he would obviously starve to death. But the beetle wasn't bothered about that. He landed with her on the biggest, greenest leaf in the tree, gave her the honey from the flowers to eat and said that she was very pretty, although she didn't look a bit like a May beetle. Afterwards, all the other May beetles living in the tree came to see them; they examined Thumbelina, and the lady beetles drew in their feelers and said, "But she's only got two legs, what a miserable sight." "She's got no feelers," said another. "She's so slender around the waist, ugh! She looks like a human being. Isn't she ugly," said all the lady beetles, even though Thumbelina was pretty. The beetle who had caught her thought she was pretty, but when all the others said she was hideous, he finally believed it as well, and decided he didn't want her. He told her she could go whenever she liked. They flew down from the tree with her and put her on a daisy. Once there, she wept because she was so ugly that the May beetles wouldn't have her, and yet she was as sweet and fair as the most beautiful rose petal.

Throughout the whole summer poor Thumbelina lived on her own in the big forest. She wove herself a bed from blades of grass and hung it under a big leaf so that it couldn't rain on her. She gathered honey from the flowers and ate it, and drank the dew that gathered on the leaves each morning. That was how the summer and autumn passed. But then winter came, the long, cold winter. All the birds that had sung so beautifully for her flew away. The trees and flowers withered and the big leaf she had been living under rolled up and turned into nothing but a dead yellow stalk. Thumbelina was terribly cold, for her clothes were torn, and she was so delicate and tiny. It seemed that she would freeze to death. It began to snow, and every snowflake that fell on her was like a whole bucketful would be to us, for she was no taller than a thumb. She wrapped herself in a withered leaf, but it didn't warm her, and she shivered with cold.

Close to the forest where she was, there was a big cornfield. The corn had been taken away long ago, and there was nothing but the bare, dry stubble sticking up from the frozen soil. To Thumbelina it was like walking through a forest, and she was shivering with cold. Then she came to a field-mouse's door. It was a little hole under the stubble. There the fieldmouse had a comfortable warm house with a whole room full of corn, a lovely kitchen and a pantry. Thumbelina went to the door like a penniless beggar girl, and asked for a little barleycorn, for she hadn't had a bite to eat for two days.

"You poor little thing," said the fieldmouse, for she was really a good old fieldmouse. "Just you come inside into my warm parlour and have a meal with me."

The fieldmouse liked Thumbelina, and so she said, "I'll let you stay here for the winter if you like, but you must keep my parlour clean and tidy, and tell me stories, for that is what I like best." And Thumbelina did as the old fieldmouse wished, and she was very happy and comfortable indeed.

"We'll soon be having a visitor," said the fieldmouse. "My neighbour usually comes to see me every day of the week. He's even better off than I am; he has some huge rooms in his house and dresses in such a lovely black velvet coat. If only you could get him as your husband, you'd be set. But he can't see. You must tell him the nicest stories you know."

But Thumbelina was not keen on that, and she certainly didn't want to marry the neighbour, for he was a mole. He visited them in his black velvet coat, and he was ever so rich and wise the fieldmouse whispered. His house was over twenty times bigger than the fieldmouse's, but he disliked the sunshine and the beautiful flowers. He said nasty things about them, for he had never seen them. Thumbelina was asked to sing, and she sang both "Ladybird, ladybird, fly away home" and "Ring-a-ring-o'-roses". The mole fell in love with her because of her beautiful voice, but he didn't say anything, for he was a very serious person.

The mole had recently dug out a long underground passageway from his own house to theirs, and he allowed the fieldmouse and Thumbelina to take a walk in it whenever they wanted. But he told them not to be afraid of the dead bird lying in the passageway. It was all there, complete with feathers and beak and it must have died quite recently at the start of winter and been buried just at the spot where the mole had made his tunnel.

THEN SHE CAME TO A FIELDMOUSE'S DOOR

The mole took a piece of touchwood in his mouth – for that shines like fire in the dark, you know – and went ahead to light the way for them in the long, dark tunnel. When they arrived at the spot where the dead bird lay, the mole turned his broad nose up towards the roof and pushed the earth up, making a big hole for the daylight to shine through. There was a dead swallow lying there, with his beautiful wings folded tight against his sides, and his legs and head drawn back in his feathers. There could be no doubt the poor bird had died of cold. Thumbelina felt terribly sorry for him. She was very fond of little birds, for they had sung and chirped so beautifully for her throughout the summer, but the mole pushed this one aside with his short legs and said, "He'll not be chirping any more now. It must be miserable to be born a little bird. Thank heaven, none of my children will be one. A bird like that can't do anything but tweet-tweet, and it's bound to starve to death in the winter."

"Yes, you're absolutely right. That's a very sensible view," said the fieldmouse. "What does such a bird get for all its proud chirping when the winter comes? It can only starve and be cold; but then that's doubtless supposed to be splendid, too."

Thumbelina said nothing, but when the others turned their backs on the bird, she bent down, pushed his head feathers aside and kissed his closed eyes. "Perhaps that's the one that sang so beautifully for me last summer," she thought. "Oh, he gave me so much pleasure, that dear, beautiful bird."

The mole closed the hole that the daylight was shining through, and accompanied the ladies home. That night Thumbelina simply couldn't sleep. She got up from her bed and wove a lovely big blanket of hay, and then she carried it down and spread it over the dead bird. She put some soft cotton that she had found in the fieldmouse's parlour along the sides of the bird to keep him warm in the cold earth.

"Goodbye, beautiful little bird," she said. "Goodbye, and thank you for your lovely singing last summer when all the trees were green and the sun was shining so warmly on us." She placed her head against the bird's breast, but suddenly had a fright, for it sounded as though something was beating inside it. It was the bird's heart. The bird was not dead, but was only hibernating, and now he had been warmed up and was coming to life again. In autumn all the swallows fly away to the warm countries, but it's said that if one of them is left behind, it gets so cold that it falls down dead and stays where it falls, and the cold snow covers it over.

Thumbelina was so frightened that she started to tremble. He was a big bird, big compared with her that is, for she was no bigger than your thumb. Still, she summoned up her courage, placed the cotton more tightly around the poor swallow, and fetched a curled mint leaf that she herself had used as a blanket, and laid it on the bird's head.

The next night she crept down to him again, and by now the bird was quite alive. But he was so exhausted that only for a brief moment could he open his eyes and see Thumbelina, who was standing with a piece of touch-wood in her hand, for she had no other torch.

"Thank you, you pretty little child," said the sick swallow. "I've been so wonderfully warmed up. I'll soon get my strength back and will be able to fly again, out in the warm sunshine."

"Oh," said Thumbelina. "It's so cold outside; it's snowing and freezing. You just stay in your warm bed, and I'll look after you."

She brought the swallow some water in a flower petal. He drank it and told her how he had scratched one of his wings on a hawthorn, so he couldn't fly as quickly as the other swallows who were leaving for warmer countries. Then, at last, he had fallen to the ground, but he couldn't remember any more and had no idea how he had got down into the tunnel.

The swallow stayed in the tunnel throughout the winter, and Thumbelina was kind to him and became very fond of him. Neither the mole nor the fieldmouse got to know the least thing about this, for they didn't like the poor little swallow, you know.

As soon as spring came and the sun's warmth penetrated the earth, the swallow said goodbye to Thumbelina, who opened the hole that the mole had made in the roof. The sun shone in on them, and the swallow asked if she would like to go with him. She could sit on his back, and they would fly far out into the green forest. But Thumbelina knew it would upset the old fieldmouse if she left in this way.

"No, I can't," said Thumbelina.

"Goodbye, goodbye, you kind, lovely child," said the swallow as he flew out into the sunshine. Thumbelina watched him go, and her eyes filled with tears, for she had become very fond of him.

"Cheep, cheep," sang the bird as he flew off into the green forest.

Thumbelina was terribly upset. She wasn't allowed to go out into the warm sunshine at all. The corn that had been sown in the field above the fieldmouse's house grew so tall that it would be like a forest to this poor little girl who was no bigger than your thumb.

"Now, this summer you must start on your trousseau," said the fieldmouse to Thumbelina, for their neighbour, the dreary mole in his black velvet coat, had asked Thumbelina to marry him. "As the mole's wife, you'll need both clothes to wear and linen for the bed."

The fieldmouse hired four spiders to help Thumbelina spin and weave night and day. Each evening the mole called on them to say that once the summer came to an end the sun wouldn't be nearly so warm, and the earth would no longer be baked as hard as brick. Yes, once the summer was past he would celebrate his wedding with Thumbelina. But she was not the least bit pleased, for she wasn't fond of the dreary mole at all. Every morning when the sun rose, and every evening when it set, she tiptoed to the door, and when the wind blew aside the tops of the cornstalks she could see the

WHEN THE WIND BLEW ASIDE THE TOPS OF
THE CORNSTALKS ...SHE COULD SEE THE BLUE SKY

blue sky, she thought how light and beautiful it was out there and wished that she could see her dear swallow again. But it would never come, for it must be flying far away in the beautiful green forest.

When autumn arrived, Thumbelina had her trousseau ready.

"In four weeks you shall celebrate your wedding," said the fieldmouse to her. But Thumbelina wept and said she didn't want the dreary mole.

"Nonsense," said the fieldmouse. "Don't be stubborn, or else I'll bite you with my sharp white teeth. You're getting such a nice husband. Not even the queen has a dress to compare with his velvet coat. He's very wealthy, let me tell you. You just thank your lucky stars."

The day of the wedding arrived, and the mole came to fetch Thumbelina. She was going to live with him deep down under the earth, and never come out into the warm sunshine, for the mole didn't like sunshine. The poor child was very upset. Now she would have to say farewell to the beautiful sunshine, which at least she'd been allowed to see from the doorway when she had lived with the fieldmouse.

"Goodbye, sunshine," she said and held her arms up high in the air, and she even stepped a little way outside the fieldmouse's house. By now the corn had been harvested, and there was nothing left but the dry stubble. "Goodbye, goodbye," she said and flung her arms around a little red flower. "Give my love to the swallow if you should see him."

Just then she heard a sound above her. "Cheep, cheep," it said. She looked up, and it was the little swallow that happened to be passing by. He was so pleased to see Thumbelina. She told him how she didn't want the ugly mole as her husband, and how she was to live deep down under the ground, where the sun never shone. She couldn't help weeping at the thought.

"Now the cold winter's coming," said the little swallow. "I'll be flying off to the warm countries. Will you come with me? You can sit on my back. Just tie yourself on with your belt, and then we'll fly away from the

THEN THE SWALLOW FLEW HIGH UP IN THE AIR

nasty mole and his dark rooms, far away across the mountains to the warm countries where the sun shines more beautifully than here, where it's always summer and the lovely flowers are always in bloom. Just you fly with me, dearest little Thumbelina, who saved my life when I lay frozen in the dark cellar under the earth."

"Yes, I'll go with you," said Thumbelina, and she climbed up on to the bird's back, with her feet out on its spreading wings, and tied her belt tightly on one of the strongest feathers. Then the swallow flew high up in the air over forests and lakes, and over the towering mountains where the snow always lies. Thumbelina froze in the cold air, but then she crept down under the bird's warm feathers and only put out her little head to see all the beauty below.

Then they came to the warm lands. The sun was shining much more brightly, the sky was twice as high, and the most wonderful green and black grapes were growing by the roadside and on fences. Lemons and oranges hung in the forests, and there was a scent of myrtle and curled mint, and pretty children were running by the roadside playing with big colourful butterflies. But the swallow flew still further, and everything became even more beautiful. There, beneath magnificent green trees by a blue lake, stood a shining white marble palace, with vines climbing up its lofty pillars. At the top of the pillars, were lots of swallows' nests, and the swallow carrying Thumbelina lived in one of them.

"This is my home," said the swallow. "But if you choose one of the splendid flowers growing down there, I'll put you on it, and you'll be able to live in as cosy a place as you could wish for."

"How lovely!" she said, clapping her tiny hands.

There was a big, white marble column lying below them. It had fallen and broken in three pieces, but in between them grew the most beautiful white flowers. The swallow flew down with Thumbelina and put her on one of the broad leaves; but what a surprise awaited her! There was a tiny man sitting in the middle of the flower, as pale and fine as though he were made of glass. He had a golden crown on his head and beautiful clear wings on his shoulders, and he was no bigger than Thumbelina. He was a flower angel. In every flower there lived a little man or woman like him, but he was king of them all.

"How handsome he is," whispered Thumbelina to the swallow. The sight of the swallow upset the little King, for it seemed gigantic to him, but when he saw Thumbelina he was happy. She was the most beautiful girl he had ever seen. And so he took his golden crown from his head and put it on hers. He asked what she was called, and then he asked her to be his wife and queen of all the flowers. Thumbelina knew that this was the husband for her, quite different from the toad's son and the mole in his black velvet coat. And so she said yes to the little King. From every flower there came a lady or gentleman, and they were all so handsome, it was a joy to behold. They each brought a present for Thumbelina, but the best of them all was a pair of beautiful wings. They were fixed to Thumbelina's back so that she, too, could fly from flower to flower. There was such rejoicing, and the little swallow sat up in his nest and sang for them as well as he knew how, and yet in his heart he was sad, for he was fond of Thumbelina and didn't want ever to be separated from her.

"You shan't be called Thumbelina," said the flower angel to her. "It's an ugly name, and you are so beautiful. We shall call you Maya."

"Goodbye, goodbye," said the little swallow, and he left the warm countries again and flew far away to Denmark, where he had a little nest above the window belonging to the man who knows how to tell fairy tales. The swallow sang for him, "Cheep! Cheep!" – and, believe it or not, that's where this story has come from.

THE NIGHTINGALE

I SUPPOSE you know that in China there was once a Chinese Emperor whose palace was the most magnificent in the world. It's many years now since this happened, but for this very reason it's worth listening to the story before we forget it! The palace was entirely and completely built of fine porcelain, ever so costly, but ever so fragile, so brittle to the touch that you really had to be careful. In the garden you could see the most wonderful flowers, and tied to the most magnificent of them all were silver bells, which rang so that you wouldn't pass by without noticing the flowers. Yes, everything in the Emperor's garden was so cleverly thought out and the garden stretched so far that not even the gardener knew where it ended. If you kept on walking, you came to the loveliest forest with tall trees and deep lakes. The forest went right down to the sea, which was blue and deep. Big ships could sail right in under the branches, and in these branches there lived a nightingale. This nightingale sang so divinely that even a poor fisherman, who was out pulling up his nets at night and had so much else to take care of, lay still and listened when he heard the nightingale. "How beautiful it is," he said, but then he had to attend to his things and forgot the bird; yet the next night when it was singing and the fisherman heard it again, he said the same thing: "How beautiful it is."

From all the countries on earth people came to visit the Emperor's city, and they admired it and the palace and the garden, but when they happened to hear the nightingale, they all said, "That is the best of it all."

The travellers talked about the nightingale when they got home, and learned people wrote many books about the city, the palace and the garden, and they always mentioned the nightingale. And those who could write poetry wrote beautiful poems, all of them about the nightingale in the forest by the deep lake.

Those books went all over the world, and of course some of them reached the Emperor. He sat on his golden chair, reading and reading and nodding his head again and again, for he was delighted to see all these magnificent descriptions of the city, the palace and the garden. "And yet the nightingale is the best of it all," they said.

"What's this?" said the Emperor. "The nightingale? I don't know anything about it. Is there such a bird in my kingdom, and even in my own garden? I've never heard that! It seems I must read books to find out about it."

And then he sent for his Lord-in-Waiting, who was so distinguished that when someone of lower rank than he took the liberty of speaking to him, he answered only "P" – and that doesn't mean anything at all.

"There's said to be a most remarkable bird here, called a nightingale," said the Emperor. "They say it's the best thing of all in my vast empire. Why has no one ever told me about it?"

"I've never heard anyone mention it before," said the Lord-in-Waiting. "It's never been presented at Court."

"I desire that it should come here this evening and sing for me," said the Emperor. "The whole world knows what I have, and I don't know."

"I've never heard any mention of it before," said the Lord-in-Waiting. "I shall look for it; I shall find it."

But where was the bird to be found? Lord-in-Waiting ran up and down all the staircases, through the halls and corridors – but none of the people he met had heard of the nightingale. So the Lord-in-Waiting ran back to the Emperor and said that it must be some story made up by those people who wrote books. "Your Imperial Majesty shouldn't believe everything that is written. It's all made up."

"I HEAR THE NIGHTINGALE SING"

"But the book in which I read about it," said the Emperor, "has been sent to me by the high and mighty Emperor of Japan, and so it can't be false. I insist on hearing the nightingale. It shall be here this evening. It shall enjoy my gracious favour. And if it doesn't come, then the entire court shall be thumped in the stomach when they've had their supper."

"Tsing-pe," said the Lord-in-Waiting, and ran again up and down all the staircases, through all the halls and corridors; and half the Court ran with him, for they were not keen on having their stomachs thumped. Everyone was asking about the remarkable nightingale that was known all over the world, but not by any of the Court.

At last they came across a poor little girl in the palace kitchens and she said: "Oh, yes, the nightingale! I know it well. My word, it can sing! Every evening I'm allowed to take a few of the scraps from the table home to my poor sick mother, who lives down near the shore. And when I walk back tired, and rest in the forest, I hear the nightingale sing. It brings tears to my eyes. It's as though my mother were kissing me."

"Little kitchen maid," said the Lord-in-Waiting. "I'll get you a better job in the kitchen and even give permission for you to watch the Emperor eat if you can take us to the nightingale, for it is summoned to appear at Court this evening."

And so the Lord-in-Waiting, the kitchen maid and half the Court went off into the forest where the nightingale usually sang. As they were walking along, a cow started to moo.

"Oh," said the courtiers. "There it is. What remarkable power there is in such a tiny creature. I'm sure I've heard it before."

"No, that's the cows mooing," said the little kitchen maid. "We are still a long way from the place."

Now the frogs began croaking down in the pond.

"Lovely," said the Chinese Court Chaplain. "Now I can hear her; it sounds just like little church bells."

"No, that's the frogs," said the little kitchen maid. "But I think we'll soon be hearing it now."

Then the nightingale began to sing.

"That's it," said the little girl. "Listen, listen. And there it is." And she pointed to a tiny grey bird up in the branches.

"Can that be?" said the Lord-in-Waiting. "I would never have imagined

—41—

it like that. How ordinary it looks. It must have lost its colour on seeing so many distinguished people around it."

"Little nightingale," called the kitchen maid loudly. "Our gracious Emperor would very much like you to sing for him."

"With the greatest pleasure," said the nightingale, and sang so sweetly, it was a delight to hear.

"It's like glass bells," said the Lord-in-Waiting. "And see its little throat – just look how it uses it. It's remarkable we have never heard it before. It will be a great success at Court."

"Am I to sing again for the Emperor?" asked the nightingale, who thought the Emperor was already present.

"My excellent little nightingale," said the Lord-in-Waiting. "It gives me great pleasure to summon you to a Court banquet this evening, when you will enchant His High Imperial Majesty with your entrancing song."

"It sounds best out here in the green forest," said the nightingale. But it willingly went along with them when it heard of the Emperor's wish.

Everything in the palace had been properly polished. The walls and floors of porcelain were shining in the light of many thousands of golden lamps. The prettiest of flowers, which could all tinkle like bells, had been placed along the corridors. People were rushing about so much that they set all the bells tinkling. You could hardly hear yourself speak.

In the middle of the great hall where the Emperor was sitting, a golden perch had been set up, and it was on this the nightingale was to sit. The entire Court was present, and the little kitchen maid had been permitted to stand behind the door, for now she had been given the title of "Proper Kitchen Maid". All were dressed in their finest clothes, and they were all looking at the little grey bird as the Emperor nodded to her to begin.

And the nightingale sang so beautifully that tears came to the Emperor's eyes and flowed down his cheeks. Then the nightingale sang even more beautifully, and its song went right to the Emperor's heart. The Emperor was so happy, he said that the nightingale should have his golden slipper to hang around its neck. But the nightingale said no thank you, as it had already been sufficiently rewarded.

"I have seen tears in the Emperor's eyes and that is the richest treasure for me; an emperor's tears have a wondrous power. I have been rewarded enough." And then it sang again in its divine voice.

"CAN THAT BE?" SAID THE LORD-IN-WAITING. "I WOULD NEVER
HAVE IMAGINED IT LIKE THAT"

"It's the most wonderful show I've ever seen," said the ladies of the Court, and they filled their mouths with water to try to warble like the nightingale. Indeed, even the lackeys and chambermaids were content, and that is saying something, for they were by far the most difficult people to impress. Yes, indeed, the nightingale was a great success.

It was decided that the nightingale was to remain at the palace and have its own cage, and it had the liberty to take a walk twice a day and once every night. It was accompanied by twelve servants, each holding tightly on to a silken ribbon tied to its leg. There wasn't much fun in those walks.

The entire city talked about the remarkable bird, and when two people met, one simply would say "Night-", and the other replied "gale", and then they would sigh and understand each other. Indeed eleven grocers' children were named after it, but not one of them could sing a note.

One day a big package arrived for the Emperor, and on the outside was written the word "Nightingale".

"Ah, we've been sent a new book about our famous bird," said the Emperor. But it was not a book; in the box there was an elaborate little contraption, an artificial nightingale that was intended to look like the real one, except that it was studded all over with diamonds, rubies, and sapphires. When the artificial bird was wound up it could sing one of the pieces sung by the real bird, and then its tail went up and down, glittering with silver and gold. Around its neck hung a little ribbon upon which were written the words: *"The Emperor of Japan's Nightingale is poor beside that of the Emperor of China."*

"How lovely," everyone said, and the person who had brought the artificial bird was immediately given the title of "Deliverer-in-Chief of the Imperial Nightingale".

Then the Emperor said "Now they must sing together. What a duet it will be!"

And so they were made to sing together, but it didn't really work, because the real nightingale sang in its own way, and the artificial bird was worked by a system of rollers. "It's not to be blamed," said the Court's music master. "It keeps extremely good time and corresponds entirely to my way of thinking." Then the artificial bird was made to sing on its own. It was admired just as much as the real one, and it was so much prettier to look at, as it sparkled like bracelets and brooches.

Thirty-three times it sang the same piece, and still it wasn't tired. People would have liked to hear it all over again, but the Emperor thought that the real nightingale should also be allowed to sing. But where was it? No one had noticed that it had flown out of the open window, away to its green forests.

"What *is* all this?" asked the Emperor. And all the courtiers grumbled and said they thought the nightingale was an extremely ungrateful creature. "But we've got the best bird," they said, and then the artificial bird was made to sing again It was the thirty-fourth time they'd heard the same piece, but they didn't know it by heart yet, for it was a difficult tune. The music master was full of praise for the bird, even saying that it was better than the real nightingale, not only because of its beautiful jewels, but also on the inside.

"You see, My Lords and Ladies, and above all the Emperor, with the real nightingale you can never work out which song is going to come next, but with the artificial bird, everything is fixed. It will always work the same way. You can explain it, you can open it up and reveal the human invention, show how the wheels are arranged, how they work, and how one thing follows on another!"

"Those were my very thoughts," everyone said, and the music master was permitted to demonstrate the bird for the people of the city the following Sunday; they, too, should hear it sing, said the Emperor. And they heard it and they were extremely pleased and they all said "oh" and nodded. But the poor fisherman who had heard the real nightingale said, "It's got a good sound to it, and there's a fair resemblance, but there's something missing, although I don't know what."

The real nightingale was exiled from the Emperor's realm; but the artificial bird had its place on a silk cushion close to the Emperor's bed. All the presents it had received, including gold and precious stones, lay around it, and its title had been raised to "Imperial Bed-table Singer-in-Chief", first in rank on the left, for the Emperor considered the side on which the heart is found to be the most distinguished, and the heart is on the left, even in an Emperor. And the music master wrote twenty-five volumes about the artificial bird; they were learned and long and filled with the most difficult words, but everyone said that they had read and understood them, for they didn't want to seem stupid.

A whole year passed. The Emperor, the Court and all the other people knew by heart every little note in the artificial bird's song, and for that very reason they thought terribly highly of it because they could join in, and so they did. Everyone from the street urchins to the Emperor sang "zizizi! cluckcluckcluck!" Yes, it was most certainly lovely.

THE ARTIFICIAL BIRD HAD ITS PLACE ON A SILK CUSHION

But one evening, just as the artificial bird was in the midst of its song and the Emperor was lying in bed listening to it, something went "svup" inside the bird; something broke, and all the wheels spun round with a "surrrrrr!", and the music stopped.

The Emperor jumped out of bed and sent for his personal physician, but what help could he give? Then he sent for the watchmaker, and after a lot of talking and checking he managed to repair the bird, but he said that it must be treated gently, for the pivots were terribly worn, and if he replaced them the music might not play properly. How sad everyone became! They let the bird sing only once a year, and even that wore it out. But then the music master gave a little speech containing lots of difficult words and said that everything was as good as before, and so everyone believed that things were as good as before.

Five years had passed, and the whole country was overtaken by a great sorrow. The Emperor was ill and it was said he wouldn't live, and they all loved their Emperor. A new emperor had already been chosen, and people stood about in the street and asked the Lord-in-Waiting how their Emperor was.

"P!" he said, shaking his head.

Cold and pale the Emperor lay in his magnificent big bed. The entire Court thought he was dead, and they all rushed off to pay their respects to the new Emperor. The chamberlains and the palace maids ran around talking to everyone about it. Drapes had been placed in all the halls and corridors so that no one should be heard walking, and so it was very quiet. But the Emperor was still not dead. Stiff and pale he lay in the magnificent bed with the long velvet curtains and the heavy gold tassels. A window was open, and the moon shone in on the Emperor and the artificial bird.

The poor Emperor could hardly draw his breath; it was as though something was sitting on his chest. He opened his eyes, and then he saw it was Death sitting on his chest, wearing his gold crown and holding the Emperor's gold sword in one hand and his magnificent banner in the other. All around in the folds of the velvet bed curtains strange faces were peering forth, some terribly ugly, others lovely and serene; they were all the Emperor's good and bad deeds, looking at him now that Death was near.

"Remember that?" they whispered one after another. "Remember that?" And then they reminded him of his past actions until beads of sweat came to his forehead.

"I don't remember," said the Emperor. "Music, music! The big Chinese drum!" he shouted, "so I don't have to listen to everything they say!"

But they continued, and Death nodded at everything that was said.

"Music, music," begged the Emperor. "You divine little golden bird. Sing, please sing! I have given you gold and precious jewels. I've personally hung my golden slipper round your neck. Please sing, sing!"

But the bird stood in silence; there was no one to wind it up, and without that it couldn't sing. But Death continued to look at the Emperor with his big, empty eyes, and everything was so quiet, so dreadfully quiet.

At that moment, close to the window, the loveliest song was heard. It was the little live nightingale sitting on the branch outside. It had heard of the Emperor's distress, and had come to sing comfort and hope to him. And as he sang, the faces became paler and paler, and the blood began to flow more and more quickly in the Emperor's weak limbs, and Death himself listened and said, "Go on, little nightingale. Go on."

At that the Emperor cried, "Then will you give me the magnificent golden sword? Then will you give me the splendid banner? Will you give me the Emperor's crown?"

And Death gave each precious thing for a song, and the nightingale went on singing, and it sang of the quiet churchyard where the white roses grow, where the elder tree spreads its scent, and where the fresh grass is watered by tears. Then Death began to long for his own garden and slipped away like a cold white mist out of the window.

"Thank you, thank you," said the Emperor. "You heavenly little bird. I drove you out of my realm, and yet you have sung away all those evil visions from my bed and removed Death from my heart. How shall I reward you?"

"You have rewarded me enough," said the nightingale. "I saw tears come to your eyes the first time I sang, and that I shall never forget. Those are jewels that gladden a singer's heart. But sleep now and be well and strong. I'll sing for you."

And it sang, and the Emperor fell into a sweet sleep, a gentle and refreshing sleep.

The sun was shining in on him through the window when he awoke, strengthened and well. His servants had not yet come back, for they thought he was dead, but the nightingale was still singing.

"You must stay with me for ever," said the Emperor. "You need only sing when you want to, and I'll break the artificial bird into a thousand pieces."

"Don't do that," said the nightingale. "It did what it could. Keep it anyway. I can't live in the palace, but let me come when I want to, and then in the evenings I'll sit on the branch over by the window and sing for you so that you can feel cheerful and thoughtful. I'll sing of happy people, and of those who are suffering. I'll sing of the good and the evil that surround you but are kept hidden from you. I fly far and wide, to the poor fisherman, to the farmer's roof, to all those people who are far from you and your Court. I love your heart more than your crown, and I'll come and I'll sing for you. But one thing you must promise me."

"Anything," said the Emperor, standing in his imperial robes, which he had put on himself, and holding up to his heart the sword that was heavy with gold.

"One thing I will ask you. Tell no one that you have a little bird that tells you everything. Things will be better that way."

And then the nightingale flew off.

So when the servants came in to see to their dead Emperor, they found him standing there, and the Emperor said "Good morning."

DEATH HIMSELF LISTENED AND SAID, "GO ON LITTLE NIGHTINGALE. GO ON"

THE PRINCESS AND THE PEA

THERE was once a prince who wanted to marry a princess, but she had to be a *real* princess. So he travelled all over the world to find one, but wherever he went there was always something wrong. There were plenty of princesses, but he couldn't be sure that they were *real* princesses, as there was always something about them that wasn't quite right. And so he went home again and was very upset, for he so much wanted to find a real princess to love.

And then, one evening, there was a terrible storm. There was thunder and lightning, and the rain came down in torrents. It was quite dreadful! In the middle of the storm there was a knock at the gate, and the old king went out to open it.

There was a princess standing outside. But heavens, what a mess she looked! There was water running down her hair and her clothes, in at the toe of her shoe and out at the heel. Still, she said she *was* a real princess.

"Well, we'll soon see about that!" thought the old queen, but she didn't say anything. She went into the bedroom, took off all the bedlinen and put a pea on the base of the bed. Then she took twenty mattresses and laid them on top of the pea, and then she took twenty quilts filled with real eiderdown and put them on top of the mattresses.

And that was to be the princess's bed for the night.

In the morning they asked her how she had slept.

"Oh, simply terribly!" said the princess. "I hardly had a wink of sleep all night! Goodness knows what was in the bed. I was lying on something hard, and I'm black and blue all over. It's simply appalling!"

And so they could see she was a real princess, for she had felt the pea through the twenty mattresses and the twenty quilts filled with eiderdown. No one could be as thin-skinned as that unless she were a proper princess.

And so the prince took her for his wife, for he knew at last that he had found a real princess. The pea was placed in the royal museum, where it can still be seen, unless someone has taken it.

"I HARDLY HAD A WINK OF SLEEP ALL NIGHT!"

THE STEADFAST TIN SOLDIER

THERE were once twenty-five tin soldiers, who were all brothers, for they had all been born from an old tin spoon. They all shouldered their rifles and stared straight ahead, and their uniforms were red and blue and looked quite splendid. The very first thing they heard in this world was when the lid was taken off the box in which they were lying and a little boy clapped his hands and shouted, "Tin soldiers!" He had been given the soldiers for his birthday, and he began to set them out on the table. Each soldier was exactly the same as the others, except for one who had only one leg, for he had been the last to be moulded, and there had not been enough tin. But he stood just as firmly on his one leg as the others on their two, and this story is about him.

There were many more toys on the table where the soldiers were placed, but what was most striking was a beautiful paper castle. Through the tiny windows you could see right into the rooms. Outside there were little trees standing around a small mirror that was supposed to look like a lake, and swimming on it and mirroring themselves were some wax swans. It was very charming, but the prettiest thing of all was a little maiden standing at the open door of the castle. She, too, was cut out of paper, but she was wearing a skirt of the finest linen and had a narrow little blue ribbon draped over her shoulder, and in the middle of the ribbon there was a sparkling sequin the size of her face. The little lady was stretching out both her arms,

THE PRETTIEST THING OF ALL WAS A LITTLE MAIDEN STANDING
AT THE OPEN DOOR OF THE CASTLE ~~~~~ SHE WAS A DANCER ~~~~~

for she was a dancer, and she was holding one leg so high that the tin soldier couldn't see where it was and thought she had only one leg, just as he had.

"She'd be just the wife for me," he thought. "But she's rather elegant. She lives in a castle, whereas I've nothing but a box, and there are twenty-five of us to share it. It's no place for her. Even so, I must see if I can get to know her." And then he stretched out behind a snuff box that was lying on the table. From there he could see the elegant little lady, who kept standing on one leg without losing her balance.

Late in the evening all the other tin soldiers were put in their box, and the people of the house went to bed. Then the toys began to play, paying visits, going to war and having a party. The tin soldiers rattled away in their box, for they wanted to join in, but they couldn't get the lid off. The nutcracker did somersaults, and the slate pencil had fun on the slate. There was such a noise that the canary woke up and joined in, chattering away in verse. The only two who didn't move were the tin soldier and the little dancer. She stood quite straight on the tips of her toes and held both her arms out wide; he was just as steady on his one leg, and not for a single moment did he take his eyes off her.

Then the clock struck twelve, and snap, the lid of the snuff box sprang open. But instead of snuff there was a little hobgoblin inside, a jack-in-the-box, and it was a clever little thing.

"Tin soldier," said the jack-in-the-box. "Will you keep your eyes to yourself?"

But the tin soldier pretended not to hear it.

"All right, just you wait till tomorrow," said the jack-in-the-box.

When morning came and the children got up, the tin soldier was placed on the window ledge; and either because of the jack-in-the-box or a draught, suddenly the window flew open and the soldier fell out head first from the third floor. It was a terrible fall; he landed on his head, with his leg up in the air, and his bayonet stuck down between the cobble stones.

The maid and the little boy went straight down to look for him, but even though they almost stepped on him, they still couldn't see him. Had the tin soldier shouted, "Here I am," they would probably have found him, but he didn't think it was proper to shout when he was in uniform.

THE BOAT SWEPT ON, FOLLOWED BY THE RAT

Soon it began to rain, and the drops fell faster and faster in a real down-pour. When the rain stopped, two ragged children appeared.

"Hey," said one of them. "There's a tin soldier over there. Let's send him for a sail."

Then they made a boat from a newspaper, put the tin soldier in the middle of it, and sent him off sailing down the gutter. The two boys ran alongside, clapping their hands. What waves there were in that gutter, and what a current there was! Well, it had been pouring with rain. The paper boat rocked up and down, and sometimes it spun around so quickly that the tin soldier quivered a little. But he stood firm, looked straight ahead and shouldered his rifle.

All of a sudden, the boat drifted into a drain covered by a long plank; it became as dark as it had been in his box.

"I wonder where I'm going now?" he thought. "Oh, it's all because of the jack-in-the-box. If only the little lady were here with me in the boat, then I wouldn't mind even if it were twice as dark."

At that moment a huge water rat that lived in the drain appeared.

"Have you got a passport?" asked the rat. "Let's have your passport."

But the tin soldier made no reply and took an even firmer grip on his rifle. The boat swept on, followed by the rat. It ground its teeth and kept shouting to all the twigs and straws:

"Stop him, stop him! He's not paid the toll! And he's not even shown his passport!"

But the current grew stronger and stronger. The tin soldier could already glimpse the daylight ahead at the end of the drain, but he could also hear a great rushing sound that was enough to frighten even the bravest man. The end of the drain gushed out into a huge canal; it would be as dangerous for him as it would be for us to sail down over a great waterfall.

He was already so near it that he couldn't stop. The boat rushed out and the poor tin soldier held himself as stiff as he could; no one could claim that he as much as blinked. The boat twirled around three or four times and filled to the top with water, so it was bound to sink. The tin soldier was standing up to his neck in water, the boat was sinking deeper and deeper, and the paper was unravelling. Then the water rose over the soldier's head – and at that moment he thought of the charming little dancer whom he would never see again, and in his mind he could hear:

> Go forth, oh warrior bold,
> With death thou aye must reckon.

Suddenly the paper broke, and the tin soldier fell through – but just then he was swallowed by a big fish.

Oh dear, how dark it was inside the fish. It was even worse than in the drain, and it was such a tight squeeze. But the tin soldier remained brave, lying stretched out, shouldering his rifle.

The fish started rushing this way and that, lurching about in a terrible manner. At last it fell quiet, and then suddenly it was as if a flash of lightning cut through it. The daylight shone brightly, and someone shouted

aloud: "Tin soldier!" The fish had been caught, taken to market and sold, and had ended up in a kitchen where a maid cut it open with a big knife. With two fingers she took hold of the soldier by the waist and carried him into the parlour, where everyone wanted to have a look at this remarkable man who had been travelling around inside a fish, though the tin soldier himself thought nothing of it. They placed him on the table and there – the strangest things do happen in this world! – the tin soldier was in the very same room where he had been before; he saw the very same children, and the toys were on the table. Among them was the lovely castle with the charming little dancer. She was still standing on one leg and had the other raised in the air: she, too, was steadfast. The soldier was moved by this, and he was on the verge of weeping tin tears, but he knew that wasn't a proper thing to do. So he looked at her, and she looked at him, but they said nothing.

At that moment one of the little boys flung the soldier into the stove without giving anyone the slightest idea why; it must have been the jack-in-the-box that was behind it.

The tin soldier was brightly lit up, and he felt terribly hot, though whether it was from the actual fire or from love, he didn't really know. The colours had drained from him, though whether this was the result of his travels or from distress, no one could tell. He looked at the little lady, and she looked at him, and he felt himself melting, but still he stood there bravely shouldering his rifle. Then a door opened, and the draught caught the dancer, and like a fairy she flew straight into the stove to the tin soldier, burst into flames and was gone. Then the tin soldier melted and turned into a tiny blob of metal, and when the maid emptied the ashes the following day, she found him in the shape of a little tin heart. But of the dancer there was nothing left except the sequin, and that was coal black from the fire.

He felt himself melting, but still he stood there

THE LITTLE MERMAID

FAR out to sea the water is as blue as the petals of the loveliest corn-flower and as clear as the purest glass, but it is very deep, deeper than any anchor rope can reach. Many church towers would have to be piled on top of each other to stretch from the bottom up to the water's surface. Down there live the sea people.

Now you certainly shouldn't think that there is nothing but bare white sand on the bottom. No, the most wondrous trees and plants grow there, and so flexible are their stalks and leaves that at the least movement of the water they sway as though they were alive. All the fishes, both big and small, dodge through the branches just like birds in the trees. In the deepest part of all lies the sea king's palace. Its walls are made of coral, and its long pointed windows of the clearest amber. But the roof is of oyster shells that open and close with the movement of the water. It looks lovely, for in each of them there is a radiant pearl, splendid enough for a queen's crown.

The sea king had been a widower for many years, but his old mother kept house for him. She was a clever woman, but proud of her noble descent, and so she went around with twelve oysters fixed on her tail, whereas other people of distinction were allowed only six. Otherwise she deserved great praise, especially because she was so fond of her little granddaughters, the sea princesses. All six were lovely children, but the youngest was the most beautiful of them all. Her skin was as clear and pure as a rose petal, her eyes as blue as the deepest sea, but like all the others, she had no feet, for her body ended in a fish tail.

All day long the princesses would play in the palace, in the great halls where living flowers grew out of the walls. The huge amber windows were open, and the fishes swam in through them, just as the swallows fly in when we open the windows in our world. The fishes swam straight across to the little princesses, ate from their hands and allowed themselves to be patted.

Outside the palace there was a big garden with fiery red and dark blue trees. Their fruits shone like gold, and their flowers like burning fire, and their stalks and leaves were constantly moving. The ground itself was the finest sand, but blue, like sulphur flames. There was a wondrous blue glow

THE SEA KING HAD BEEN A WIDOWER FOR MANY YEARS

over everything down there, and you might think that you were high up in
the air, seeing nothing but the sky above and below you, rather than that
you were on the bottom of the sea. In calm weather you could just glimpse
the sun, which looked like a crimson flower with all the light radiating from
its centre.

Each of the princesses had her little patch in the garden, where she could
dig and plant as she wanted. One of them fashioned her patch of flowers in
the shape of a whale, another preferred hers to look like a little mermaid,
but the youngest made hers quite round like the sun, and in it she grew
only flowers that shone red like the sun. She was a curious child, quiet and
reflective, and when the other sisters decorated their gardens with the most
wonderful things they had found in sunken ships, all she wanted, apart from
the rose-coloured flowers that looked like the sun, was a beautiful marble
statue of a lovely boy. It was carved out of clear white stone, and it had
sunk to the bottom after a shipwreck. Near the statue she planted a rose-
coloured weeping willow, which grew splendidly. Its fresh branches hung
over the statue, down towards the blue sea bed where its shadow fell violet
and moved with the branches. It looked as though the top and the roots
were playing at kissing each other.

No joy was greater to the youngest princess than hearing about the
human world above. Her old grandmother had to tell her everything she
knew about ships and cities, people and animals, and it seemed especially
wonderful to her that up on earth the flowers were scented – for they

ALL SHE WANTED . . . WAS A BEAUTIFUL MARBLE STATUE OF A LOVELY BOY

weren't down here on the sea-bed – that the forests were green, and the fish you could see on their branches could sing so loud and beautifully that it was a delight to hear them. The grandmother said fishes instead of birds, or they wouldn't have understood her, as they had never seen a bird.

"When you are all fifteen," said their grandmother, "you will be allowed to go up to the top of the sea and sit on the rocks in the moonlight. You can watch the big ships sailing past and you'll see forests and cities." The following year one of the sisters reached her fifteenth birthday, but each princess was a year younger than the next, and so the youngest of them still had a whole five years to wait before she was allowed to go up from the bottom of the sea to see what it was like in our world. But each promised the next one to tell her what she had seen and found most beautiful on the first day. Their grandmother couldn't tell them enough, and there was so much they had to find out about.

None of them was as filled with longing as the youngest, who had the longest to wait, and who was so quiet and thoughtful. Many nights she stood by the open window and looked up through the dark blue waters, where the fish were flipping their fins and tails. She could see the moon and the stars, although they shone very palely, but through the water they looked far bigger than they do to our eyes. If something like a black cloud glided beneath them, then she knew that it was either a whale swimming above her, or else a ship full of people, who scarcely thought that a lovely little mermaid was standing below them stretching up her hands towards the keel.

Now that the eldest princess was fifteen, she was allowed to go up to the surface, and when she came back she had a hundred and one things to tell. The most beautiful thing of all, she said, was to lie in the moonlight on a sandbank in a calm sea, and watch the big city near the coast with lights twinkling like hundreds of stars, to hear the music and all the noise and din of carriages and people and see all the church towers and spires, and hear the bells ringing. And just because she couldn't go any closer, that was what she longed for most of all.

Oh, how the youngest sister listened, and afterwards, when she stood by her open window in the evening gazing up through the dark blue water, she thought of the big city with all the noise and din, and she imagined she could hear the church bells ringing down to her.

The following year, the second sister was allowed to rise up through the water and swim wherever she wanted. She came to the surface just as the sun was setting, and she thought that this was the most beautiful thing of all. The entire sky had looked like gold, she said, and as for the clouds, she just couldn't sufficiently describe their beauty. They had been red and violet as they drifted over her, but far faster than the clouds, like a long white veil, a flock of wild swans had flown over the water against the setting sun. She swam towards the sun, but it sank, and the pink glow on the sea and the clouds vanished.

The following year the third sister went up. She was the boldest of them all, and so she swam right up a broad river running out to sea. She saw lovely green hills covered with vines, and palaces and farms peered out from among magnificent forests. She heard all the birds singing, and the sun shone so warmly that she often had to dive down under the water to cool her burning face. In one small bay she came across a whole crowd of little children, who were running about naked and splashing in the water. She wanted to play with them, but they ran off in fear, and a little black animal came along. It was a dog, but she had never before seen a dog. It barked at her so fiercely that she grew afraid and made her way out to the open sea, but she would never be able to forget the magnificent forests, the green hills and the pretty children who could swim in the water even though they didn't have fish tails.

The fourth sister was not so bold. She stayed far out in the wild ocean, and told them that that was the loveliest thing of all. You could see for miles around, and the sky above looked like a huge glass dome. She had seen ships, but they had been far away and looked like gulls. The dolphins had turned somersaults, and the big whales had blown water up through their nostrils, so that it had looked like hundreds of fountains.

Then it was the fifth sister's turn. Her birthday was in the winter, and so she saw what the others had not seen on their first trips. The sea looked quite green, and there were huge blocks of ice floating about. They all looked like pearls, she said, and they were far bigger than the church towers human beings built. They appeared in the most wonderful shapes, and shone like diamonds. She had sat down on one of the biggest, and all the sailing ships had been afraid and kept well away from where she was sitting with the wind blowing in her long hair. But later in the evening the sky clouded over; it thundered and lightninged, while the black sea raised the enormous blocks of ice high up so that they glistened in the red flashes of light. The terrified crews furled the sails on all the ships but the mermaid sat

She came across a whole crowd of little children

"GOODBYE," SHE SAID, AND ROSE UP THROUGH THE WATER

quietly there on her piece of ice and watched the lightning zigzagging down into the shining sea.

The first time each of the sisters went above the water they were always delighted at the beautiful new things they saw. But now that they were grown up and allowed to go up when they wanted, it was no longer particularly interesting to them. They would long to get back home, and after a month had passed they said that the most beautiful place of all was down in their world, as it felt so nice and cozy.

On many evenings the five sisters went arm in arm and swam in a row up to the surface. They had lovely voices, more beautiful than any human being, and when a storm was brewing and they thought that ships were sure to be wrecked, they swam in front of them and sang beautifully about how lovely it was on the bottom of the sea, and told the sailors not to be afraid of going down there. But the sailors couldn't understand what they said, as they thought it was the noise of the storm. Nor did they ever see how beautiful it was down there, for when a ship sank, those on board were drowned and never arrived at the sea king's palace.

When the sisters linked their arms and rose up through the sea, the youngest sister was left behind, watching them go. She looked as though she were going to weep, but a mermaid has no tears, and so she suffers far more than humans.

"Oh, if only I were fifteen," she said. "I know I shall come to love the world up there and the people who live in it."

Then at last her fifteenth birthday came.

"There, now you're off our hands," said her grandmother, the old queen mother. "Come along now, let me make you look pretty, like your sisters." She put a wreath of white lilies in her hair, but each of the flower petals was half a pearl. Then the old woman fixed eight big oysters on the princess's tail to show her high rank.

"It does hurt so," said the little mermaid.

"Yes, but everyone knows you have to suffer if you want to look nice," said her grandmother.

The youngest mermaid would have loved to shake off all this finery and put the heavy wreath aside. Her red flowers out in the garden suited her far better, but all the same she was afraid to change things. "Goodbye," she said, and rose as light and clear as a bubble up through the water.

The sun had just set when she raised her head above the sea, but all the clouds were still shining like roses and gold, and up there in the pale pink air the evening star was shining clear and beautiful. The air was mild and fresh, and the sea was as calm as a mill pond. A big three-masted ship lay close by, although only one sail was hoisted, for there was not a breath of air, and there were sailors sitting about in the rigging and on the yard-arms. There was music and singing, and as the evening grew darker, hundreds of many-coloured lanterns were lit. It looked as though the flags of all nations were billowing in the air. The little mermaid swam right up to the cabin porthole, and every time she was lifted up by the water she could see in through the panes of crystal glass. There were lots of splendidly dressed people standing there, but the most handsome of them all was a young prince with big dark eyes, who couldn't have been much more than sixteen. It was his birthday, and that is why all the fuss was being made. The sailors were dancing on the deck, and when the young prince came out, over a hundred rockets shot up in the air and lit up the scene like bright daylight, so that the little mermaid became quite frightened and disappeared under the water. But soon she popped her head up again, and then it seemed as if all the stars in the heavens were falling down on her. Never had she seen such a firework display. Great suns were spinning round, magnificent fiery fishes were swishing around in the blue air, and it was all brilliantly reflected in the clear, motionless sea. The ship itself was so bright that she could see every little bit of rope, and all the people. Oh, how handsome the young prince was, and he shook hands with his guests, and laughed and smiled as the music rang out in the lovely night.

It grew late, but the little mermaid could not take her eyes off the ship and the handsome prince. The colourful lights were put out, the rockets no longer rose up in the air, and no more cannon shots resounded, but deep down in the sea there was a rumbling and mumbling. She sat on the water, rocking up and down so that she could look into the cabin, but the ship increased its speed. Sail after sail was unfurled, and then there was more movement in the waves. Great clouds gathered, and lightning could be seen in the distance. There was going to be a dreadful storm. So the sailors rolled up the sails. The great ship was moving at enormous speed, pitching and tossing on the tempestuous sea. The waters rose like huge black mountains about to crash down on the mast, but the ship dipped down like a swan

A BIG : THREE - MASTED : SHIP :
LAY : CLOSE : BY :

among the towering waves and was raised up again on the mountainous seas. To the little mermaid this was simply great fun, but it wasn't to the sailors. Their ship creaked and cracked, the thick planks were smashed in by the powerful pounding, the sea got into the ship, the mast snapped like a reed, and the ship leaned over on its side as the water made its way into the hull. Now the little mermaid saw that the sailors were in danger, and she herself had to watch out for beams and wreckage from the ship floating on the water. One moment it was so pitch dark that she couldn't see the least little thing, but when the lightning came, it again became so clear that she could recognize everyone on the ship. They were all coping as best they could. She watched especially for the young prince, and she saw him just as the ship split in two and sank in the deep sea. At first she was quite delighted, for now he was going down into her realm, but then she remembered that human beings couldn't live under water, and that he could only go down to her father's palace as a dead man. No, she would not let him die, and she swam out among the beams and planks floating about on the sea, completely forgetting that they could crush her. She dived deep down under the water and came up again at the top of the towering waves, and finally she reached the young prince who could scarcely swim any longer in the stormy sea. His arms and legs were beginning to tire, and his beautiful eyes were closed. He would surely have died if the little mermaid had not come to his rescue. She held his head above the water and then let the waves carry her with him wherever they wanted.

When morning came the storm had passed, and there was no trace of the ship. The sun rose brilliant red and radiant from the waters, and seemed to bring life to the prince's cheeks, but his eyes remained closed. The mermaid kissed his high forehead and smoothed his wet hair. She thought he was like the marble statue down in her little garden, and she kissed him again and wished that he might live.

She saw land ahead, tall blue mountains whose peaks glistened with white snow as though swans were nesting there. Down by the coast there were lovely green forests, and in front of them lay a church or a convent: she was not sure which, but a building it certainly was. Lemon and orange trees were growing in the garden, and tall palm trees stood before the gateway. Here the sea formed a little bay, where the water was quite calm, but very deep, right up to where the fine white sand had been washed up. She swam there with the handsome prince and laid him on the sand, taking special care to make sure that his head lay in the warm sunshine.

The bells in the big white building rang out, and a crowd of girls came out through the garden. On noticing this, the little mermaid swam further out behind some high rocks jutting out of the water, and she covered her head with sea foam so that no one could glimpse her little face, and then she watched to see who would come to the poor prince.

It wasn't long before a girl went over to him. She seemed quite fright-

SHE HELD HIS HEAD ABOVE THE WATER

ened, but only for a moment, and then she fetched some of the other girls. The mermaid saw the prince come to life and smile at everyone around him, although he didn't smile out to her, for of course he didn't know she'd saved him. She felt very upset, and when he was taken into the big building she dived sadly down into the water and made her way back to her father's palace.

She had always been quiet and thoughtful, but now she became even more so. Her sisters asked her what she had seen on her first time above the surface, but she didn't tell them anything.

Many evenings and mornings she went up to the spot where she had left the prince. She saw the fruits in the garden ripening and being plucked, and she saw the snow melt in the high mountains, but she didn't see the prince, and so she was always even more upset when she went home. Her only consolation was to sit in her little garden and throw her arms around the beautiful marble statue that looked like the prince. But she didn't tend her flowers, and they grew in great confusion across the paths and entwined their long stalks and leaves in the branches of the trees in such a tangle that it became quite dark.

At last she could stand it no more, and told one of her sisters. She told the others, but then no one else was told except a couple of other mermaids, who didn't tell anyone except their closest friends. One of them knew who the prince was, and she, too, had seen the finery on the ship and knew where he came from and where his kingdom was.

"Come along, little sister," said the other princesses, and with their arms around each other's shoulders they rose in a long row to the surface of the sea close to where the prince's palace stood.

It was built of a shiny, light yellow stone, with big flights of marble steps, one of them going right down to the sea. Magnificent gilded domes rose above the roof, and between the columns all round the building there were marble statues that looked as though they were alive. Through the crystal glass in the tall windows you could see the most magnificent halls hung with costly silk curtains and rugs, and all the walls were adorned with big paintings which were a delight to behold. In the middle of the biggest hall a big fountain was playing. The jets from it rose high towards the glass dome in the ceiling through which the sun shone on the water and on the lovely plants growing in the big pool.

Now she knew where he lived, and many an evening and night she went there, and she swam much closer to land than any of the others had dared. She even went right up in the narrow canal beneath the magnificent marble balcony that cast a long shadow across the water. Here she sat looking at the young prince who thought he was alone in the clear moonlight.

Many times she saw him sailing with his musicians in his magnificent boat, with its flags waving. She peered out from among the green reeds, and if the wind caught her long silver-white veil and anyone saw it, they thought it was a swan stretching its wings.

Many nights when the fishermen lay with their torches on the sea, she heard them telling each other many good things about the young prince, and she was so pleased to have saved his life when he was drifting about half dead on the waves. She thought how firmly his head had rested on her shoulder, and how tenderly she had kissed him. He knew nothing at all of this, of course, and could not even dream of her.

She grew more and more fond of human beings, and more and more she wished that she could rise up and join them. It seemed to her that their world was far bigger than hers, for they could fly across the sea in ships, climb the lofty mountains high above the clouds, and the countries they owned stretched, with forests and fields, further than she could see. There were so many things she would like to know, but her sisters couldn't give her an answer to them all. So she asked her old grandmother, about the lands above the sea.

"If human beings don't drown," asked the little mermaid, "do they live for ever then? Don't they die, as we do down here in the sea?"

"Yes," said the old woman. "They too must die, and their lives are even shorter than ours. We can live to be three hundred, but then, when our lives come to an end, we simply change into foam on the water, and we don't even have a grave down here among our loved ones. We have no immortal soul; there's no more life for us. We are like the green reeds which once they've been cut down can't turn green again. Human beings, on the other hand, have a soul that lives for ever, after their bodies have turned to earth. It rises up through the clear air, up to all the shining stars. Just as we rise up from the sea and see the lands of human beings, so they rise up to unknown beautiful places that we are never allowed to see."

"Why were we never given an immortal soul?" said the little mermaid, in distress. "I would give all the three hundred years I have to live, just to be a human being for a single day and then have my share of the heavenly world."

"You mustn't think like that," said the old grandmother. "We have far better and happier lives than the human beings up there."

"So I must die and float like foam on the sea, without hearing the music of the waves or seeing the lovely flowers and the red sun. Can't I do anything, then, to gain an eternal soul?"

"No", said the old woman. "Only if a human being were to love you so much that you meant more to him than his father and mother. Only if he clung to you with all his heart and all his mind, and married you with his right hand in yours with a promise of faithfulness now and to all eternity. Then his soul would flow into you, and then you, too, could have your share of human happiness. He would give you a soul and still keep his own. But that can never happen. The very thing that is so beautiful here in the sea, your fish tail, they find ugly up on earth, because they know no better. Up there they must have two clumsy supports that they call legs, in order to be beautiful."

Then the little mermaid sighed deeply and gave her fish tail a look of great distress.

"Let's enjoy ourselves," said the old grandmother. "Let's hop and dance throughout the three hundred years we have to live. It's quite a long time, you know. After that we can pass on with all the more contentment. We're going to have a court ball this evening!"

The ball was more splendid than anything ever seen on earth. The walls and ceiling in the great dance hall were made of thick, clear glass. Several hundred colossal mussel shells, rose pink and grass green, were arranged in rows on either side, and a burning blue fire illuminated the entire hall and shone out through the walls so that the sea outside was completely lit up. You could see all the countless fish, great and small, swimming towards the glass wall; the scales on some of them purple, on others silver and gold. A broad flowing stream ran through the midst of the hall, and in this mermen and mermaids danced to the accompaniment of their own lovely singing. No one on earth has such a beautiful voice. The little mermaid sang most beautifully of them all, and they clapped their hands for her, and for a moment she felt joy in her heart, for she knew that she had the most beautiful voice of all on earth and in the sea. But she couldn't forget the handsome prince and her sorrow at not being able to have an immortal soul, as he did. And so she crept out of her father's palace, and while all was singing and enjoyment inside, she sat sadly in her little garden. Then suddenly she heard horns resounding down through the water, and she thought, "He's sailing up there, I'm sure, the man I love more than my father and mother, the man at the centre of all my thoughts, and into whose hands I would entrust all my life's happiness. I'll risk everything to win him and an immortal soul. While my sisters are dancing in my father's palace, I'll go to see the sea witch. I've always been afraid of her, but perhaps she can give me advice and help me."

The little mermaid went out of her garden towards the roaring whirlpools behind which the witch lived. She had never gone that way before. There were no flowers growing there, no sea grass, only the bare grey bed of sand stretched out towards the whirlpools where the water, like rushing mill wheels, swirled around and dragged everything within reach down into the depths. She knew she had to go between these grinding whirlpools to reach the place where the sea witch lived, and for a long way the only path led her across some warm, bubbling mud which the witch called her peat bog. Beyond it lay the witch's house in the middle of a strange forest. All the trees and bushes were half beast and half plant, and they looked like snakes with a hundred heads growing out of the earth. All their branches were long, slimy arms, with fingers like wriggling worms, and joint by joint they were moving from their roots to their uttermost tips. They twined themselves round anything they could catch hold of in the sea, and they never let it go. The little mermaid became quite frightened standing out there; her heart was pounding with fear, and she was on the point of turning back, but then she thought of the prince and the human soul, and she gathered up courage. She tied her long flowing hair tight round her head so that the beasts in the forest wouldn't be able to grab hold of it, then she folded both hands on her chest, and in this way, like a fish, she darted off through the water, in between the dreadful beasts reaching out for her with their curling arms and fingers. She saw that every one of them was holding on to something it had caught; hundreds of little arms were clinging on to things like strong bands of iron. Human beings who had drowned at sea and sunk to the bottom here, were peeping like white skeletons from the arms of the beasts. Ships' rudders and treasure chests they held, and skeletons of land animals, and a little mermaid they had caught and strangled – that seemed the most dreadful thing of all.

Now she came to a big, slimy open space in the forest, where big, fat water snakes were playing and showing their ugly whitish-yellow bellies. In the middle of the open space a house had been built with the white bones of shipwrecked sailors, and there sat the sea witch, with a toad eating from her mouth in just the same way as people let canaries eat sugar from their lips. She called the horrible fat water snakes her little chicks and let them play about on her big spongy chest.

"I know what you want, all right," said the sea witch. "It's a silly thing you're doing. But even so, you shall have your will, for it will bring you misfortune, my lovely princess. You want to get rid of your fish tail and instead have two stumps to walk on like human beings so that the young prince can fall in love with you and you can have him and an immortal soul." And as she said this the witch laughed so loudly and horribly that the toad and the sea snakes fell writhing to the ground. "You've come at just the right time," said the witch. "Tomorrow, when the sun rises, I wouldn't be able to do anything for you for another year. I'll make a potion for you. Before the sun rises you must swim to land, sit down on the shore and drink it. Then your tail will divide and shrink in to what human beings call legs. But it'll hurt, as though sharp swords are slicing through you. Everyone who sees you will say you are the most beautiful creature they've ever seen. You will still have your graceful poise. No dancer will move so elegantly, but every step you take will be as though you are treading on a knife so sharp that it will bring blood. If you're willing to suffer all this, then I'll help you."

"Yes," said the little mermaid in a trembling voice, thinking of the prince and of winning an immortal soul.

"But remember," said the witch, "once you have taken human shape, you can never again become a mermaid. You will never be able to go down through the water to your sisters and your father's palace. If you don't win the prince's love, so that he forgets his father and mother for you and cherishes you with all his being and takes you as his wife, then you won't get an immortal soul. The first morning after he marries someone else, your heart will break, and you will turn to foam on the water."

"That's what I want," said the little mermaid, turning deathly pale.

"But you must also pay me," said the witch. "And it is no small thing I demand. You have the loveliest voice of all down here at the bottom of the sea. You think you'll be able to entrance him with that, but you must give that voice to me. For my precious potion I want the best thing you possess. I shall have to put my own blood in it for you, you see, so that the potion can become as keen as a double-edged sword."

"But when you take my voice," said the little mermaid, "what shall I have left?"

"Your beautiful figure," said the witch, "your graceful poise and your expressive eyes. With those you'll be able to entrance a human heart. Well, have you lost your courage? Put your little tongue out, and I'll cut it out in payment, and you shall have the potion."

"So be it," said the little mermaid, and the witch put on the cauldron to boil the magic potion. "Cleanliness is a good thing," she said, wiping out the cauldron with the snakes tied in a knot; then she scratched herself and let her black blood drip down into it. The steam produced such fantastic shapes that anyone would be frightened. The witch kept putting fresh things in the cauldron, and when it was boiling properly it made a sound like crocodiles weeping. At last the potion was ready; it looked like the purest water.

"Here you are," said the witch, taking out the little mermaid's tongue, and from then on the little mermaid could neither sing nor speak.

"If the beasts should grab at you when you go back through my forest," said the witch, "just sprinkle a single drop of this potion on them, and their arms and fingers will break into a thousand pieces." But the little mermaid didn't need to do that. The beasts drew back from her in terror when they saw the shining potion glistening in her hand like a star. And so she soon got back through the forest, the marsh and the roaring whirlpools.

She could see her father's palace. The torches had been put out in the great dance hall, so they were probably all asleep in there, but still she did not dare to look for them, now that she could not speak and was about to leave them for ever. It was as though her heart would break with grief. She crept down into the garden, took one flower from each of her sisters' flower-beds, blew a thousand kisses towards the palace and rose up through the dark blue sea.

The sun had not yet risen when she saw the prince's palace and went up the magnificent marble steps. The moon was shining, beautiful and clear. The little mermaid drank the burning sharp potion, and it was as if a two-edged sword went through her delicate body. She fainted and lay as though dead. When the sun began to shine on the sea she awoke to feel a searing pain, but just in front of her stood the handsome young prince with, his coal black eyes fixed on her. She looked down and discovered that her fish tail was gone, and that she had the prettiest legs any girl could have, but she was quite naked, and so she wrapped herself in her thick long hair. The prince asked who she was and how she had got there, and she looked at him tenderly and yet so sadly with her dark blue eyes, for she couldn't speak. Then he took her by the hand and led her into the palace. Every step she took was, as the witch had said already, as though she were treading on sharp knives, but she suffered it gladly. Holding the prince by the hand she rose as light as a bubble, and he and everyone else were amazed at her lovely, graceful poise.

THEY SAW THE SHINING POTION GLISTENING IN HER HAND

They dressed her in costly garments of silk and muslin. In the palace she was the most beautiful of all, but she could neither sing nor speak. Lovely dancing girls, clad in silk and gold, came out and sang for the prince and his royal parents. One of them sang more beautifully than all the others, and the prince clapped his hands and smiled at her, and then the little mermaid was sad, for she knew that she herself had sung far more beautifully still. She thought, "Oh, if only he knew that to be with him I have given away my voice for all eternity."

The dancing girls performed a lovely, graceful dance to the most glorious music, and then the little mermaid raised her beautiful white arms, got up on the tips of her toes and floated across the floor, dancing as no one had danced before. At every exquisite movement her beauty became yet more apparent, and her eyes spoke more deeply to the heart than did the song of the dancing girls.

Everyone was entranced by this, especially the prince, who called her his little foundling. She danced more and more, although every time her foot touched the earth it was as though she were treading on sharp knives. The prince said that she should be with him always, and she was allowed to sleep near him on a velvet cushion.

He had clothes made for her so that she could go riding with him. They rode through the scented forests where the green branches touched her shoulders and the little birds sang behind the fresh leaves. Together with the prince she climbed the high mountains, and although her delicate feet bled, she laughed it off and they climbed until they saw the clouds floating beneath them like a flock of birds flying off to foreign lands.

At home in the prince's palace, while the others were asleep at night, she went out on the broad marble steps, and cooled her burning feet in the cold sea water, and then she thought of her home down there in the depths.

One night her sisters came up arm in arm. They sang sorrowfully as they swam along in the water, and she waved to them, and they recognized her and told her how sad she had made them all. After that they visited her each night. Then, one night, far out among the waves, she saw her old grandmother, who had not been up above the water for many years. The sea king was there, too, wearing his crown. They stretched their arms out to her, but didn't dare come as close to the land as the sisters.

Day by day, the prince grew fonder of the little mermaid. He loved her

JUST IN FRONT OF HER STOOD THE HANDSOME YOUNG PRINCE

SHE FLOATED ACROSS THE FLOOR, DANCING AS NO ONE HAD DANCED BEFORE

as one can love a good, dear child, but it never occurred to him to make her his queen. Yet she knew that she had to become his wife, for otherwise she would never have a soul, and on the morning after his wedding she would turn into foam on the water.

"Don't you love me most of all?" the little mermaid's eyes seemed to say when he took her in his arms and kissed her beautiful forehead.

"Yes indeed, you are the one I love most," said the prince. "For you have the kindest heart of them all. You are the one who is most devoted to me, and you look like a young girl I once saw but shall probably never find. A ship I was sailing on was wrecked, and the waves carried me ashore near a sacred temple, where several young girls were serving. The youngest of them found me near the shore and saved my life. I only saw her twice, but she is the only one I could love in this world. You look very like her – you almost force her image out of my soul. She belongs to the sacred temple, and so my good fortune has sent you to me, and we shall never part."

"Alas, he doesn't know that I saved his life," thought the little mermaid. "I carried him over the sea to the forest where the temple stands. I sat behind the foam and kept watch to see whether anyone would come. I saw the beautiful girl that he loves more than he loves me." And the mermaid sighed deeply; she couldn't weep. "The girl belongs to the sacred temple, he says. She'll never come out into the world, and they'll never meet again. But I'm with him, and see him every day, and I'll tend him, love him, sacrifice my life for him."

But soon people began to say that the prince was to marry and have the neighbouring king's daughter as his wife, and that was why he was preparing such a magnificent ship. "The prince is going away to see the neighbouring king's lands," they said. "But it's really to see the neighbouring king's daughter, and he's taking a great retinue with him." But the little mermaid shook her head and laughed. She knew the prince's thoughts far better than anyone else. "I must go away," he had said to her. "I must go and see the beautiful princess. My parents insist, but they shall not force me to bring her home as my bride. I can't love her. She isn't like the girl in the temple, the one whom you resemble. If I were to choose a bride, I would rather choose you, my silent foundling with talking eyes." And he kissed her red lips, stroked her long hair and laid his head at her heart so that she dreamt of human happiness and an immortal soul.

"But do you mean to say you're not afraid of the sea, my silent child?" he said as they stood on the magnificent ship that was to carry him to the neighbouring king's land. He told her of storms and of being becalmed, and about strange fish deep down in the water, and of what the diver had seen down there, and she smiled at what he said, for she knew about the bottom of the sea better than anyone else.

In the moonlit night, when all were asleep except the first mate, who was standing at the helm, she sat by the ship's railings, staring down through the clear water, and it seemed to her that she glimpsed her father's palace. Her old grandmother was standing at the top of it with a silver crown on her head, staring up through the swirling waters towards the keel of the ship. Then her sisters appeared over the water, and they stared mournfully at her and wrung their hands. She waved to them, smiled and wanted to tell them that everything was going well for her, but the ship's boy came along, and the sisters dived down so that he thought that what he had seen was foam on the sea.

The following morning the ship docked in the neighbouring kingdom. All the church bells were ringing, and trumpets were blown from the lofty towers while the soldiers stood with waving banners and glittering bayonets. There was a feast every day. Balls and receptions followed one after the other, but the princess was not there yet. She was being educated far away in a sacred temple, they said, where she was learning all the royal virtues. At last she arrived.

The little mermaid was eager to see her beauty, and she had to acknowledge that she had never seen a more charming creature. Her skin was fine, and behind the dark eyelashes smiled a pair of dark blue, faithful eyes.

"It's you," said the prince. "You who saved me when I lay like a dead man on the shore." And he held his blushing bride tight. "Oh, I am so happy," he said to the little mermaid. "The best thing of all, the thing I never dared hope for, has happened to me. You will rejoice in my happiness, for you love me most of all." And the little mermaid kissed his hand, and she seemed already to feel her heart breaking. For the morning after his wedding would bring death to her and change her into foam on the sea.

All the church bells sounded, and the heralds rode about in the streets announcing the engagement. On all the altars sweet-smelling oils burned in silver lamps. The priests swung their censers, and bride and bridegroom held out their hands to each other and were given the bishop's blessing. The little mermaid was dressed in silk and gold and held the bride's train, but her ears didn't hear the festive music, and her eyes didn't see the sacred ceremony. She was thinking of her death, and of everything she had lost in this world.

That very same evening the bride and bridegroom went on board ship. The cannon sounded, all the flags waved, and in the middle of the ship stood a tent of gold and purple filled with lovely cushions. This was where the couple were to sleep in the quiet, cool night.

The sails billowed in the breeze, and the ship glided light and steady across the clear ocean.

When darkness fell, colourful lanterns were lit, and the sailors danced merry dances on the deck. The little mermaid couldn't help thinking of the first time she appeared above the sea and saw the same splendour and joy, and she whirled around in the dance, gliding as a swallow glides when it's being pursued, and everyone cried out in admiration of her, for never had she danced so marvellously. It was as if sharp knives were cutting her delicate feet, but she didn't feel it; the wound in her heart was far more painful. She knew it was the last evening she would see the man for whom she had left her family and her home, sacrificed her lovely voice and each day endured endless torment without his having had the slightest idea. It was the last night she would breathe the same air as he, see the deep sea and the starry blue sky. Instead an everlasting night without thoughts or dreams awaited her, this mermaid who had no soul and could never win one. All was joy and merriment on the ship until long past midnight. The mermaid laughed and danced with the thought of death in her heart. The prince kissed his lovely bride, and she caressed his black hair, and arm in arm they went to rest in the magnificent tent.

Silence fell on the ship, and only the first mate stood at the helm. The little mermaid laid her arms on the railing and looked for the morning glow in the east. She knew that the first ray of the sun would kill her. Then she saw her sisters rise up from the sea. They were pale like her, and their beautiful long hair was no longer fluttering in the wind: it had been cut off.

"We've given it to the witch to get her to help so you won't have to die tonight. She's given us a knife – here it is. Do you see how sharp it is? Before the sun rises you must plunge it into the prince's heart, and then, when his warm blood splashes on your feet, they will grow together into a fish tail, and you'll become a mermaid and you can come down into the water to us and live your three hundred years before you're turned into salt sea foam. Hurry! Either he or you must die before the sun rises. Our old grandmother is so upset that her white hair has fallen out, just as ours fell beneath the witch's scissors. Kill the prince and come back. Hurry – can you see the touch of red in the sky? The sun will rise in a few minutes, and then you must die." And they gave a strange deep sigh and sank beneath the waves.

The little mermaid drew the purple curtain back from the tent, and she saw the lovely bride sleeping with her head on the prince's chest. Kneeling down, she kissed his beautiful forehead. She glanced at the sky where the glow of morning was shining more strongly, then she glanced at the sharp

knife and fixed her eyes on the prince, who in his dreams was whispering
the name of his bride: she alone was in his thoughts. The knife trembled in
the mermaid's hand – but then she threw it far out into the waves. A red
sheen spread over the place where it fell, as though drops of blood were
bubbling up through the water. Once more she looked at the prince
through half-glazed eyes, then she threw herself from the ship down into
the sea, and she felt her body dissolve into foam.

The sun rose from the sea. Its rays fell warm and gentle on the cold sea
foam, and the little mermaid had no sense of death. She saw the clear sun,
and up above her hovered hundreds of beautiful transparent creatures
through whom she could see the white sails of the ship and the red clouds
in the sky. Their voices were melodious, but so delicate that no human ear
could hear them, and no earthly eye could see them. They were so light
they floated in the air without wings. The little mermaid saw that she had a
body like theirs, and it was rising higher and higher up from the foam.

"To whom am I coming?" she said, and her voice sounded like those of
the other creatures, so ethereal that no earthly music can recreate it.

"To the daughters of the air," they answered. "A mermaid can never
have an immortal soul unless she wins the love of a human being. Her eternal life depends on someone else. The daughters of the air do not have eternal souls, but through good deeds they can create them. We fly to the
warm lands where the sultry plague-ridden air can kill, and we fan them
with cool breezes. We fill the air with the scent of flowers, and bring
refreshment and healing. When we have striven for three hundred years to
do the good we can, we are given an immortal soul and eternal bliss. You,
poor little mermaid, with all your heart have striven to do the same as we.
You have suffered and endured, raised yourself to the realm of the spirits of
the air, and now, through good deeds, you too can create an immortal soul
for yourself."

And the little mermaid stretched her clear arms up towards the sun, and
for the first time she felt tears. On the ship there was once more noise and
bustle. She saw the prince and his beautiful bride looking for her, and they
stared sadly at the bubbling foam, as though they knew she had thrown herself into the waves. Unseen, she kissed the bride's forehead, smiled to the
prince and rose up with the other children of the air, up on to the rose-
coloured cloud floating above.

SHE ROSE UP WITH THE OTHER CHILDREN OF THE AIR

THE TINDERBOX

ONCE there was a soldier marching along a road. He had a pack on his back and a sword at his side, for he had been to war, and now he was on his way home. He met an old witch on the road. She was very ugly and her lower lip hung right down over her chin. She said, "Good evening, soldier. My word, what a nice sword and a big pack you've got. You're a true soldier. Now you shall have as much money as you want."

"Thank you, old witch," said the soldier.

"Do you see that big tree?" said the witch, pointing to one beside them. "It's hollow inside. You must climb to the top, and there you'll find a hole that you can slide through to get right down into the tree. I'll tie a rope round your waist so I can pull you up again when you shout."

"What am I to do down in the tree?" asked the soldier.

"Fetch money," said the witch. "Now listen: when you get down to the bottom of the tree, you'll be standing in a big passageway. It's quite light, for there are over a hundred lamps burning there. Then you'll see three doors. You can open them, for the keys are in the locks. If you go into the first room, you'll find a big chest in the middle of the floor, and a dog sitting on top of it. He's got eyes as big as teacups, but you needn't worry about that. I'll give you my blue chequered apron to spread out on the floor. Go quickly across, take the dog and put him on my apron, then open the chest and take as many pennies as you want. They are all made of copper, but if you'd rather have silver you must go into the next room. There's a dog there with eyes as big as mill-wheels, but you needn't worry about that. Just put him on my apron and help yourself to the money. On the other hand, if you want gold, you can have as much of that as you want if you go into the third room. But the dog on the money chest in there has eyes as big as the Leaning Tower of Pisa. That's some dog, believe me! But you needn't worry at all about that. Just put him on my apron, and he'll not harm you, and you can take as much gold from the chest as you want."

"That's not a bad idea," said the soldier. "But what am I to give you, old witch? I imagine you want me to bring you something or other."

"No," said the witch. "Not a single penny do I want. All you have to do

HE MET AN OLD WITCH ON THE ROAD

for me is to bring back an old tinderbox that my grandmother forgot the last time she was down there."

"All right then. Let's put the rope around my waist," said the soldier.

"Here we are," said the witch. "And here's my blue chequered apron."

The soldier climbed up into the tree and let himself drop down in the hole, and then, as the witch had said, he was standing in a long passageway where many hundreds of lamps were burning.

He opened the first door. There sat the dog with eyes as big as teacups, staring at him.

"You're a fine dog," said the soldier, placing him on the witch's apron and taking as many copper coins as he could cram into his pocket. Then he closed the chest, put the dog back on it and went into the second room. There was the dog with eyes as big as mill-wheels.

"You shouldn't look at me like that," said the soldier. "You might get an eye-ache." And then he put the dog on the witch's apron. But when he saw all those silver coins in the chest, he threw away all the copper coins he already had and filled his pockets and his pack with nothing but silver. And then he went into the third room. Oh dear, it was horrible! The dog in there really had eyes as big as the Leaning Tower of Pisa – and they were spinning round and round in his head like wheels.

"Good evening," said the soldier, touching his cap, for never before had he seen such a dog as this. But when he'd looked at the dog for a short while he felt brave enough to lift him down on the floor and open the chest. Oh my, what a lot of gold there was! He'd be able to buy the whole of Copenhagen and all the cakes and sugar pigs, and all the tin soldiers and rocking horses in the world. That was a lot of money! And the soldier threw away all the silver coins he had filled his pockets and pack with, and took gold instead until all his pockets, his pack, his cap and his boots were filled and he could hardly walk. He had so much money! He put the dog back on the chest, slammed the door and then shouted up through the tree:

"Now pull me up, old witch!"

"Have you got the tinderbox?" asked the witch.

"Oh, that's right," said the soldier. "I'd quite forgotten it." And he went back and fetched it. The witch pulled him up, and he found himself on the road again, with his pockets, boots, pack and cap full of money.

THERE SAT THE DOG WITH EYES AS BIG AS TEACUPS

"What do you want with that tinderbox?" asked the soldier.

"That's no concern of yours," said the witch. "You've got your money. Just give me the tinderbox."

"Nonsense," said the soldier. "Tell me what you want it for, or else I'll draw my sword and chop your head off."

"No," said the witch.

So the soldier chopped off her head. Then he wrapped up all his money in her apron, slung the bundle on his back, put the tinderbox in his pocket and went on to the town.

It was a magnificent place, and he went to the best inn and demanded the very best rooms and his favourite food, for now he was very rich.

The servant who polished his boots that evening thought they were pretty peculiar old boots for such a rich gentleman. But the following day the soldier bought himself some new boots and some nice clothes. Now the soldier had become a fine gentleman, and the townspeople told him about all the splendid things there were in their town, and about their king, and what a pretty princess the King's daughter was.

"Where can I see her?" asked the soldier.

"She can't be seen at all," they all said. "She lives in a big copper castle surrounded by many walls and towers. No one but the king is allowed to go and visit her, because it has been predicted that she'll marry a perfectly ordinary soldier, and that's something the king doesn't want."

"I'd very much like to see her," thought the soldier, but of course he would never be permitted to do so.

The days passed and the soldier amused himself by going to the theatre, driving through the royal park and giving lots of money to the poor – and that was nice of him. He knew from the old days how awful it was to be penniless. Now he was rich and had nice clothes, and he made many friends who told him what a nice person he was, and that he was a real gentleman, and the soldier liked that very much. But as he was always spending his money, he soon had only two coins left and had to move out of the beautiful rooms he'd been living in, up into a tiny room right under the roof. He had to polish his own boots and repair them with an old needle, and none of his friends came to see him, because there were so many stairs to climb.

One very dark evening, he realized that he couldn't even buy himself a candle, but then it dawned him that there was a stump of one in the tinderbox he had taken from the hollow tree. He took out the tinderbox and the stump of candle, and he struck a light. Sparks flew from the flint, the door flew open, and the dog with eyes as big as teacups, that he'd seen down beneath the tree, stood before him, and said, "What is my master's wish?"

"What's going on?" said the soldier. "This is a strange tinderbox, if I can have anything I want just like that! Get me some money," he said to the dog, and whoosh! it was gone, and whoosh! it was back, holding a big bag of coins in its mouth.

Now the soldier realized what a wonderful tinderbox this was. If he struck it once, along came the dog from the chest of copper coins. If he struck it twice, along came the dog with the silver coins, and if he struck it three times the dog in charge of the gold appeared. That day the soldier moved back into the beautiful rooms and put on his expensive clothes again, and all his friends recognized him, and began to visit him again.

Then one day the soldier thought: "How strange it is that you can't get to see that princess. She's supposed to be so lovely. But what's the good of that when she spends all her time in that big copper castle with all those towers? Can't I get to see her at all? Where's my tinderbox? And then he struck the tinderbox once, and whoosh, the dog with eyes as big as teacups appeared.

"I know it's the middle of the night," said the soldier, "but I would love to see the princess, just for a moment."

The dog immediately disappeared through the door, and before the soldier had time to gather his thoughts, the dog came back with the princess. She was sound asleep on the dog's back and was so lovely that anyone could see she was a real princess. The soldier simply couldn't help it — he had to kiss her, for he was a real soldier.

Then the dog ran back with the princess, but when morning came and the king and queen were pouring the tea, the princess said that she had had a strange dream about a dog and a soldier. She had ridden on the dog's back, and the soldier had kissed her.

"That's a nice story," said the queen. Then she told one of her ladies-in-waiting to keep watch by the princess's bed the following night to see whether it was a real dream, or whether it was something else.

The soldier longed to see the lovely princess again, and so the dog came back the next night, took the princess and ran away as fast as he could. But the old lady-in-waiting put on her boots and ran just as fast after them. When she saw them disappear into a big house, she thought, "Now I know where it is," and with a piece of chalk she drew a big mark on the gate. Then she went home and back to bed. Soon after, the dog came along, with the princess. But when he saw that a mark had been drawn on the gate where the soldier was living, he took a piece of chalk and drew marks on all the gates in the town. That was a clever thing to do, for the lady-in-waiting wouldn't be able to find the right gate, of course, if there were marks on all of them.

Early the next morning the king and queen, the old lady-in-waiting and all the officers went out to find where the princess had been taken.

"There it is!" said the king as he saw the first gate with a mark on it.

"No, dear, it's there," said the queen, who had noticed another gate that also had a mark.

"But there's one there, and one there," they all said. Wherever they looked there were marks on the gates, and they realized that it was no use looking any further.

SHE WAS SOUND ASLEEP ON THE DOG'S BACK

The queen was a very wise woman who knew a thing or two. Taking her big golden scissors, she cut a piece of silk, from which she made a little bag. She filled the bag with fine little buckwheat grains, and then she tied it on the princess's back. When that was done, she cut a hole in the bag so that the grains could trickle out all along the road taken by the princess.

The following night the dog came again, took the princess on his back and ran off with her to the soldier. He loved her very much and wished he'd been a prince so he could have her for his wife.

The dog didn't notice the grains trickling out all the way from the castle to the soldier's window, where he ran up the wall with the princess. In the morning the king and queen could see quite plainly where their daughter had been, and they took the soldier and put him in the dungeon.

Inside the dungeon it was dark and dreary, and then the king said to the soldier, "You're going to be hanged tomorrow," which wasn't a nice thing to hear. The soldier had left his tinderbox at home in the inn. In the morning he could see through the iron bars of his little window how people were hurrying to the town to see him hanged. He heard the drums and saw the soldiers marching. Everyone was rushing to watch, including a shoemaker's apprentice with a leather apron and slippers on. He was galloping along at such a speed that one of his slippers flew off just near the wall where the soldier was peeping out between the iron bars.

"Hey, shoemaker boy. You needn't hurry so much," the soldier said to him. "Nothing's going to happen until I get there. So could you just pop across to where I used to live and fetch me my tinderbox. I'll give you four coins. But you'll have to be quick." The shoemaker boy was keen to have the four coins and he ran off to fetch the tinderbox. He gave it to the soldier and – well, you'll never guess what happened next!

Outside the town a big gallows had been built, and around it were standing the soldiers and many hundreds of thousands of people. The king and queen were sitting on a throne opposite the judge and the entire council.

The soldier was standing on the ladder. When they tried to put the noose around his neck, he said that criminals were always allowed one last wish before their punishment, and that he would like to smoke a pipe of tobacco, as it would be the last pipe he ever smoked.

The king didn't object, and so the soldier took his tinderbox and struck a light once, twice, three times. There stood all the dogs: the one with the

eyes as big as teacups, the one with the eyes like mill-wheels, and the one that had eyes as big as the Leaning Tower of Pisa.

"Don't let them hang me," cried the soldier, and the dogs rushed at the judges and the council, grabbed one by the legs and one by the nose and flung them high up in the air.

"Not me!" cried the king, but the biggest dog took both him and the queen and threw them up after all the others. Then the soldiers ran away, and all the people shouted, "Little soldier, you shall be our king and marry the lovely princess."

Then they put the soldier in the king's coach, and all three dogs danced before it and shouted "Hurrah," and the children whistled through their fingers, and the soldiers waved their swords. And at last the princess came out of her copper castle to marry the soldier. The wedding lasted for a whole week, and the dogs sat at table and opened their eyes wide.

THE LITTLE MATCH GIRL

IT was dreadfully cold. It was snowing, and darkness was falling on the last evening of the year, New Year's Eve. And in this cold and darkness a poor little girl with bare feet and nothing on her head was walking along the street. She had been wearing slippers when she left home, but they were very big slippers. Her mother had been the last to use them, and they were so big that the little girl had lost them when hurrying across the street as two carriages had been driving past at an awful speed. One of the slippers was nowhere to be seen, and a boy ran off with the other, saying he could use it as a cradle when he had children of his own.

So now the little girl was walking along on tiny bare feet that were red and blue with cold. She was holding a bundle of matches in her old apron, and she had some in her hand. No one had bought any from her all day long. No one had given her a penny, and hungry and chilled to the bone, she walked along looking very sad. The snowflakes were falling on her long golden hair that curled beautifully around her neck, but she scarcely gave it a thought. In all the windows candles were shining, and there was a lovely smell of roast goose in the street. It was New Year's Eve, and that was something to which she did give a thought.

In a corner between two houses, one of them sticking a little further into the street than the other, the little girl sat down and huddled up. She pulled her legs up under her, but she became even colder, and she didn't dare go home, for she hadn't sold any matches or received a single penny. Her father would beat her, and besides it was cold at home, too. They had no more than the roof over their heads, and the wind whistled through it even though the worst cracks had been stuffed with straw and rags. Her tiny hands were almost numb with cold. Then she thought that a little match might help a bit. If only she dared take one from the bundle, strike it against the wall and warm her fingers. She pulled one out – "pshsh" – how it sputtered, how it burned! It was a warm, clear flame, just like a little candle when she held her hand around it, and a curious candle it was. It seemed to the little girl that she was sitting in front of a big iron stove with

SHE WAS SITTING UNDER THE LOVELIEST CHRISTMAS TREE

shiny brass knobs, and the fire was burning divinely, and gave out a wonderful warmth. The little girl was stretching out her feet as if to warm them, too, but then the flame died and the stove vanished. There she sat with a little stump of the burned-out match in her hand.

She struck a fresh match. It burned brightly, and the wall became transparent, like a piece of gauze, where the glow shone on it. She could see straight into a parlour, where the table was laid with a shining white cloth and fine porcelain, and there was a roast goose stuffed with prunes and apples, steaming deliciously. And what was even more splendid was that the goose jumped off the dish and waddled across the floor with a knife and fork sticking out of it, right across to the poor girl. Then the match went out, and there was nothing to be seen but the thick, cold wall.

She lit another match. Then she was sitting under the loveliest Christmas tree, which was even bigger and more gloriously decorated than the one she had once seen through the glass door at the house of a rich merchant. Thousands of candles were burning on the green branches, and many-coloured ornaments like those decorating the shop windows were looking down on her. The little child stretched out both her hands – and then the match went out. But all the Christmas candles rose higher and higher until she could see that they were the night stars. One of them fell, making a long fiery streak in the sky.

"Someone's dying," said the little girl. Her old grandmother, who was the only person ever to have been kind to her, but who was dead now, had said that when a star falls, a soul is on its way up to God.

She struck another match against the wall. It shone all around, and in the glow stood her old grandmother, so clear, so radiant, gentle and sublime.

"Grandma!" shouted the little girl. "Oh, take me with you. I know you'll have gone when the match goes out – gone like the warm stove, the lovely roast goose and the wonderful big Christmas tree." She hurried to strike the rest of the matches in the bundle, because she wanted to keep her grandmother. And the matches shone with such radiance that it was brighter than daylight. Never before had grandmother been so beautiful and so big. She lifted the little girl up in her arms, and in radiance and joy they flew, so high, ever so high. Now there was no cold, no hunger, no fear – they were with God.

But in the corner near the house in that cold morning hour sat the little

"GRANDMA!" SHOUTED THE LITTLE GIRL. "OH TAKE ME WITH YOU"

girl with red cheeks and a smile on her lips – frozen to death on the last evening of the old year. New Year's morning dawned over the little body sitting there with the matches, of which one bundle had almost all been burned. "She must have wanted to warm herself," they said. No one knew what beautiful things she had seen, or in what radiance she and her grandmother had entered into the joy of the New Year.

THE UGLY DUCKLING

IT WAS so lovely out in the countryside. It was summertime and the corn was standing yellow, and the oats green. The hay had been stacked down in the green meadows, and there a stork was walking about on its long red legs and talking to itself. The fields and meadows were surrounded by great forests, and in the midst of the forests there were deep lakes. Yes, indeed, it was lovely out in the countryside. In the sunniest spot stood an old mansion surrounded by a deep moat, and all the way from the wall down to the water's edge there grew plants so tall that little children could stand upright under the biggest of them. There were as few pathways there as in the thickest forest, and down there a duck was sitting on her nest. She was going to hatch her little ducklings, but by now she was getting bored because it was taking so long, and she rarely had visitors. The other ducks were more interested in swimming around in the moat than coming to sit under a dock leaf to have a chat with her.

At last the eggs cracked open one after the other: "Cheep! Cheep!" they went. It was as if the eggs had come to life as one after the other of the tiny ducklings stuck their heads out.

"Quack, quack. Snap, snap," said the mother duck. "Snap out of it, snap out of it." And they snapped out of it as quickly as they could, looking all around them under the green leaves, and their mother let them look as much as they wanted, for she thought that green was good for their eyes.

"Oh, isn't the world big?" said all the little ducklings, for now they had far more room than they had had inside their eggs.

"Do you think that's the whole world?" said their mother. "The world goes a long way beyond the other side of the garden, right into the parson's field. Though even I've never been as far as that. But you are all here, aren't you?" She stood up. "No, I haven't got them all. The biggest egg's still there. How long's it going to take? Oh dear, I'm getting tired of this." And she settled down again.

"Well, how's it going?" asked an old duck who had come to see her.

"One of the eggs is taking a very long time," said the sitting duck. "It won't crack. But look at the others. They're the loveliest ducklings I've ever seen. They're all the living image of their father."

IN THE SUNNIEST SPOT STOOD
AN OLD MANSION

At last—crack—and "peep, peep," chirped the little one, and out he crept. "He is big and ugly," thought Mrs. Duck. "I fear he's a turkey after all, but we'll soon see about that."

"Let me see the egg that won't crack," said the old duck. "I'll bet it's a turkey egg. I was once fooled like that, too, and I had such worries and problems with those chicks, because they're afraid of the water. I couldn't get them into it. I snapped and quacked, but it was no good. Let's see the egg. Yes, I knew it, it's a turkey egg. Just you leave it alone and teach the other children to swim."

"I'll sit on it a little longer, even so," said the duck. "I've sat on it so long that I might as well stay for a bit longer."

"All right, do as you like," said the old duck, and off she went.

At last the huge egg cracked. "Cheep, cheep," said the little one as it toppled out. He was awfully big and ugly. The duck looked at him: "He's a terribly big duckling, this one," she said. "None of the others looks like that. Surely it isn't a turkey chick. Oh well, we'll soon see. Into the water he goes, even if I have to push him in myself."

There was beautiful weather the next day. The sun shone on all the green leaves. The mother duck with all her family went down to the moat. Splash! she jumped into the water. "Quickly, follow me," she said, and the ducklings jumped in one by one. Their heads disappeared under the water, but they soon came up again and floated along beautifully and their legs moved of their own accord. They were all in the water, and even the ugly grey chick was swimming along with them.

"No, that's no turkey," said the mother duck. "Just look how beautifully he's using his legs, and how straight he's holding himself. That's my own, all right. And actually he's quite handsome, when you look at him properly. Quack, quack. Come along with me now, and I'll take you out into the world and introduce you in the duckyard. But stay close to me all the time so that no one treads on you, and watch out for the cats."

And so they went into the duckyard. There was a dreadful din in there, for there were two families fighting over a fish head, which in the end the cat ran off with.

"There, that's the way of the world," said the mother duck, licking her bill, for she would have liked the fish head, too. "Use your legs, now," she said. "Be quick, and bow your head to the old duck over there, she's the most distinguished of all of them here. She's got Spanish blood in her veins, and she's a little stout, and notice that she's got a red rag round her leg. That's something very splendid, the finest mark of distinction any duck can have as it means no one wants to get rid of her, and that she shall be acknowledged by beast and man. Now, don't turn your toes in. A well-brought-up duckling keeps its feet well apart, like its mother and father. There now. Bow your heads and say quack."

And so they did. But the other ducks looked at them and said out loud: "Just look. Now we've got to have that noisy family here as well. As though there weren't enough of us already. And just look what that one duckling looks like. We're not going to put up with him." And one duck flew across and bit the big grey chick on the neck.

"Leave him alone," said his mother. "He's not hurting anyone."

"Yes, but he's too big and strange," said the duck that had bitten him. "So he deserves it."

"You've got some pretty children, madam," said the old duck with the rag round her leg. "All except one, and he's a failure. I wish you could have that one over again."

"That can't be done, Your Grace," said the mother duck. "He's not pretty, but he's very good-natured, and he can swim as beautifully as any of the others. In fact I think I dare say even a little better. I'm sure he's going to be handsome when he's a bit older, and in time he'll perhaps not be so big. He was in his egg too long, so he isn't the right shape." And she preened the chick's neck and smoothed his feathers down. "Besides, I think he'll be strong," she said. "He'll be all right."

"The other ducklings are delightful," said the old duck. "Make yourselves at home now, but if you should find a tasty morsel like a fish head you may bring it to me."

And so they felt at home. But the poor duckling that had been the last out of the egg and looked so ugly was bitten, shoved and teased, by ducks and hens alike. "He's too big," they all said, and the turkey cock, who thought he was an emperor, puffed himself up like a ship in full sail, went straight up to the big chick and gobbled away until he was all red in the face. The poor duckling hardly knew where to turn; he was heartbroken because he was so ugly, and was the laughing stock of the entire duckyard.

That was how it went the first day, and afterwards it got worse and worse. The poor duckling was hated by everyone. His own brothers and sisters were nasty with him, and would say, "If only the cat would take you, you ugly wretch." And even his mother would say, "I wish you were miles away from here." And the ducks bit him, and the hens pecked at him, and the maid feeding the animals kicked at him with her foot.

At last the ugly duckling ran off and flew over the hedge. The little birds in the bushes flew up in alarm. "That's because I'm so ugly," thought the duckling and closed his eyes, but he kept on running until he came to the great marsh where the wild ducks lived. Here he lay all night, and he was very tired and sad.

THE POOR DUCKLING WAS HATED BY EVERYONE

In the morning the wild ducks flew up and took a look at their new companion. "What sort of a bird are you?" they asked, and the duckling turned round and greeted them as best he could.

"You are extraordinarily ugly," said the wild ducks. "But that doesn't matter to us as long as you don't marry into our family." Poor thing, he had certainly no thought of marrying, but wanted only to be allowed to lie in the reeds and drink some of the marsh water.

There he lay for two whole days. Then two wild geese, or rather wild ganders, for they were he-geese, came along. It wasn't many hours since they had hatched out, so they were rather pleased with themselves.

"Hi, friend," they said. "You're so ugly we rather like you. Drift along with us and be a bird of passage. In another marsh not far away, there are some sweet, adorable wild geese, all of them unmarried, and they can all say quack. You'd be quite a success, you're so ugly."

"Bang! Crack!" a sound rang out above them, and both the wild ganders fell dead in the reeds. Bang! Crack! came the sound again, and hosts of wild geese flew up from the reeds, and then more firing was heard. There was a great shoot under way, and hunters were all round the marsh. Some were up in the branches of the trees, hanging out over the reeds. Clouds of blue smoke rose among the dark trees and hung in the air far out across the water. The gun dogs loped out into the mud, splish, splash, and the reeds swayed in all directions. It was a terrifying experience for the poor duckling, and it turned its head around to get it down under its wing. At that very moment a dreadful big dog came up to him with its tongue hanging out and its eyes shining horribly. It came closer to the duckling with its jaws wide open, showing its sharp teeth – but then it went away again without hurting him.

"Oh, thank Heaven," sighed the duckling. "I'm so ugly that not even the dog can be bothered with me."

Then he lay quite still, while shots whistled about in the reeds, and gun after gun was fired.

It was late in the day before it became quiet, but the poor chick still didn't dare get up. He waited several hours before looking around, and then he scurried away from the marsh as fast as he could. He ran across fields and meadows, and the wind was so strong that he could hardly move against it.

Towards evening he reached a poor farmer's cottage. It was so run down that it couldn't make its mind up which way to fall, and so it remained standing. The wind was whistling around the duckling so hard that he had to keep sitting on his tail to avoid being blown away, and it got worse and worse. Then he noticed that the door had come off one of its hinges and was hanging so crookedly that he could slip into the kitchen through the crack. And so he did.

An old woman lived here with her cat and her hen, and the cat, which she called Sunny Boy, could arch its back and purr. You could even make his fur crackle, but then you had to stroke him the wrong way. The hen had stumpy little legs, and so she was called "Stumpy". She was a good egg-layer, and the old woman was as fond of her as if she were her child.

In the morning they immediately noticed the unfamiliar duckling, and the cat began to purr and the hen to cluck.

"What's this?" said the old woman, looking around. But her eyes were not good, and so she thought that the duckling was a plump duck that had got lost. "That's a nice catch," she said. "Now I can have some duck eggs, as long as it's not a drake. We'll see."

And so the duckling was allowed to stay for three weeks, but of course no eggs came. The cat was master of the house, and the hen was the mistress, and they were always saying, "We and the world!" as if they believed that they were half of it, and the better half at that. The duckling thought that other people would probably disagree, but the hen wouldn't hear of it.

"Can you lay eggs?" she asked.

"No."

"Then keep quiet."

And the cat said, "Can you arch your back and purr and make your fur crackle?"

"No."

"Then you've no right to have an opinion when sensible people are talking."

The duckling sat in a corner and felt very sad. Then he happened to think of fresh air and sunshine, and he became so overwhelmed by such a powerful and curious urge to float on the water, that at last he couldn't help telling the hen.

"What's come over you?" she asked. "You're bored, and that's why you get all these silly ideas. Lay some eggs or purr, and they'll go away again."

"But it's so nice to float on the water," said the duckling. "Such fun to get it over your head and dive down to the bottom."

"Oh yes, that's great fun, I'm sure," said the hen. "I think you've gone crazy. Ask the cat — he's the wisest creature I know — whether he likes floating on the water or diving to the bottom. You can even ask our mistress, the old woman; there's no one wiser than she in the whole world. Do you think she wants to float and get her head under water?"

"You don't understand me," said the duckling.

"Well, if we don't understand you, who will then? Surely you don't pretend to be wiser than the cat and the old woman, not to mention me? Don't take on such airs, child, and be thankful for all the kindness you've met. Haven't you been given a place in a warm room and found friends you can learn from? But you're a dimwit, and you're no fun. I shall teach you plenty of truths, because that's what friends are for. Just you get on with laying eggs and learning to purr."

"I think I want to go out into the wide world," said the duckling.

"Yes, you do that," said the hen.

And so off the duckling went. He floated on the water and he dived to the bottom, but he was ignored by every animal he came across because he was so ugly.

Soon autumn came. The leaves in the forest turned yellow and brown, and the wind took hold of them and sent them dancing all over the place. The air had a cold look to it, and the clouds hung heavy with hail and snow, and on the fence a raven stood screeching "Caw! caw!" because he was so very cold. It makes you shiver merely to think of it. The poor duckling wasn't having a very good time.

One evening when there was a gorgeous sunset, a whole flock of beautiful big birds flew out of the bushes. The duckling had never seen anything so beautiful. They were a radiant white and had long willowy necks. They were swans, and they uttered a wondrous call, spread out their magnificent

"CAN YOU LAY EGGS?" SHE ASKED

long wings and flew off from the cold regions to warmer lands and ice-free lakes. They rose high in the air, and the little ugly duckling had a strange feeling. He turned round in the water like a wheel, stretched his neck high in the air after them, and uttered a cry so loud and wondrous that he scared himself. He couldn't forget those lovely birds, and as soon as he could no longer glimpse them, he was so excited that he dived down to the bottom, and then surfaced again. He didn't know what the birds were called or where they were flying, but he loved them as he had never loved anyone else. He was not at all envious of them, for he never thought that he could wish for such loveliness himself. He would be happy if the birds would simply put up with his company. The poor, ugly creature!

Winter came and was very, very cold. The duckling had to swim around in the water to stop it freezing over completely. But every night the hole in which he was swimming became smaller and smaller, and the ice froze so hard that it crackled; the duckling had to keep paddling all the time so that the water couldn't freeze right over. At last he was worn out, and he lay quite still and was soon frozen fast in the ice.

Early in the morning a farmer came along. He saw the duckling, and broke the ice with his boot, and then took him home to his wife. There the duckling was brought back to life.

The children wanted to play with him, but the duckling thought they wanted to hurt him, and in terror he flew up into the milk bowl, splashing the milk all over the room. The farmer's wife shrieked and flung her hands up, and then the duckling flew into the trough where the butter was, and then into the flour bin and out again. What a mess he looked! The farmer's wife screamed and hit out at him with the fire tongs, and the children knocked each other over in their eagerness to catch the duckling, and they laughed and they shouted. Luckily the door was open, and out he rushed out of the house through the freshly fallen snow and into the bushes, where he lay as though in a daze.

It would be far too sad to tell of all the suffering and misery he had to endure that hard winter. But one day the duckling was lying in the marsh among the reeds when the sun began to shine warmly again, and the larks were singing. It was springtime.

The duckling suddenly stretched his wings, and noticed there was more strength in them than there used to be, and they bore him along more powerfully. And before he really knew where he was, he found himself in a

great garden where apple trees were in blossom and lilac smelled sweetly and hung on long green branches right down to the winding canals. And just in front of him, out of the thickets, came three lovely, white swans. They ruffled their feathers and floated quite lightly on the water. The duckling recognized the magnificent creatures and was overcome by a strange feeling of sadness.

"I'll fly across to those birds, those regal creatures, even though they will peck me to death because I am so ugly, yet I dare to approach them. But that doesn't matter. Better to be killed by them than to be pecked at by the ducks, snapped at by the hens, kicked by the maid looking after the duck-yard, and suffering hardship in the winter." And he flew into the water and swam towards the magnificent swans. They saw him, ruffled their feathers and moved towards him. The poor creature bowed his head towards the surface of the water and waited. But what did he see in the clear water? Beneath him he saw his own image, but it was no longer that of a clumsy, dark grey bird, ugly and repulsive – he himself was a swan. For even though he was born in the duckyard, he had come out of a swan's egg, and was a swan.

The duckling felt truly happy at all the suffering and hardship he had gone through. Now he could really appreciate his good fortune. And the big swans swam around him and stroked him with their bills.

Some little children came out into the garden, and they threw some bread and corn into the water. The smallest one shouted, "There's a new one," and the other children cried out in delight, "Yes, a new one's arrived," and they clapped their hands and danced around. They ran in to fetch their mother and father, and they threw bread and cake into the water, and they all said, "The new one's the prettiest; it's so young and lovely." And the old swans bowed before the new swan.

It made him feel quite shy and he hid his head behind his wings; he didn't know what to think. He was far, far too happy, but not the least bit proud, for a good heart can never be proud. He thought of how he had been teased and humiliated and now was hearing everyone say that he was the loveliest of all the birds. The lilacs bent their boughs down to the water before him, and the sun shone warmly, and then he ruffled his feathers and raised his slender neck and rejoiced with all his heart that he had found happiness beyond his wildest dreams.

"THE NEW ONE'S THE PRETTIEST"

ILLUSTRATORS AND SOURCES

Anne Anderson, *Hans Andersen's Fairy Stories* (1924) 15, 58, 64, 78, 81

Honor C. Appleton, *Fairy Tales* (1922) 52 (top), 70, 105

Maxwell Armfield, *Faery Tales from Hans Andersen* (1910) Front cover, 33, 54, 55, 73, 107

Mabel Lucie Attwell, *Hans Andersen's Fairy Tales* (1914) 29, 57, 92, 93, 116

Eleanor Vere Boyle, *Fairy Tales* (1872) 23, 35

Harry Clarke, *Fairy Tales* (1916) 25, 47, 86, 95

Rie Cramer and Lilian Amy Govey, *Hans Andersen's Fairy Stories* (1921) 30

Edmund Dulac, *Stories from Hans Andersen* (1911) 17, 19, 43, 51, 53, 63, 75, 83, 85

Jeannie Harbour, *Hans Andersen's Stories* (1932) Frontispiece, back cover

John Hassall, *The Ugly Duckling* (1932) 115, 119

E. A. Lemann, *Fairy Tales* (1893) 22 (bottom)

Elizabeth MacKinstry, *Andersen's Fairy Tales* (1933) 60

Kay Nielsen, *Fairy Tales* (1924) 40, 61, 99

Arthur Rackham, *Fairy Tales* (1932) 20, 21, 56, 66, 69, 96, 103

Agnes Richardson, *Stories from Hans Andersen* (1920) 102

Charles, Thomas and William Heath Robinson, *Fairy Tales from Hans Christian Andersen* (1901) 112

William Heath Robinson, *Hans Andersen's Fairy Tales* (1913) 14, 34, 36, 38, 45, 48, 52 (bottom), 62, 65, 67, 77, 91, 106, 111, 113, 117

Hester Sainsbury, *Tales from Hans Andersen* (1929) 22 (top)

Margaret W. Tarrant, *Fairy Tales from Hans Christian Andersen* (1917) 27, 37, 44, 101

T. van Hoijtema, *The Ugly Duckling* (1894) 108

Hans Andersen photographed c. 1860, reading his stories, 1